LET'S PLAY

BY

JOHN C. DALGLISH

2015

LET'S PLAY

PROLOGUE

Darrel Chase took off his black horn-rimmed glasses and rubbed a dirty sleeve across the sweat falling into his eyes. Even though it was April first, the heat in south Texas had already begun, promising a brutal summer. No shade was to be found in the small cemetery on the edge of San Antonio, and even though he'd scheduled the exhumation for early morning, it was still hot.

Darrel had served as the Medical Examiner in Hondo, Texas, for seven years and had enjoyed the experience. However, a short stint at the San Antonio morgue, filling in for Dr. Leonard Davis, had revealed bigger challenges to be tackled. When Captain John Patton had called and offered him a full-time job, on the recommendation of Doc Davis, Darrel had jumped at it.

In taking the position of Assistant

Medical Examiner, Darrel knew he would be in for some duties like the one he was on this morning. Low man on the totem pole had to do some of the stuff that the big dog didn't want to. In Hondo, he didn't have someone else to send out, and always covered these sorts of things himself. But that didn't mean he had to like it.

Attending the exhumation with him were a backhoe operator and a funeral director. The backhoe guy gave a thumbs-up to the funeral director, not bothering to try yelling over the machine. The director, a large man in khakis and a cheap dress shirt, was holding a clipboard as he came lumbering over to where Darrel stood. He looked even more uncomfortable than Darrel, already sweating through his polyester shirt, and panting as he walked.

"Nathan says he's ready."

"Okay." Darrel looked down at his own clipboard, then at the headstone, before reading aloud the information. "Section 12, Plot 23, Grave 6."

The funeral director's head bobbed up and down. "Confirmed."

Darrel continued. "Jacob Samuel Moore, interned December 22, last year."

Another head bob. "Confirmed."

"Okay, you're set to go. Tell the backhoe guy he can start digging."

3

LET'S PLAY

"Will do." The big man retraced his steps over to the large yellow machine, and signaled the go-ahead.

Darrel stepped back and watched as the backhoe began scraping the ground away from over the coffin. Looking down at the permit, he noted it had been obtained by a Mrs. Moore from Iowa, who wanted her husband buried in their joint plot near Des Moines. It wasn't terribly uncommon to have these requests granted, and it was the seventh time Darrel had been the State's legal representative.

Within a short time, the top of the coffin was exposed and the dirt along the sides was being scraped away. The wife wasn't present, as was common with exhumations, but she would be waiting back at the funeral parlor. Darrel's main purpose for being here was to make sure they didn't dig up the wrong body.

The back hoe operator got off the machine and connected some chains to the coffin, then hooked them to his bucket, before returning to his seat. Slowly, the large box rose from the ground, wobbling from side to side as it broke free from the dirt. The operator rotated the bucket to one side, moving the coffin over to where both Darrel and the funeral director could see the top.

4

A small plate attached to the lid bore a name and date carved into it. Darrel read it aloud.

"Jacob Samuel Moore."

"Jacob Samuel Moore; confirmed," the funeral director responded.

"Okay, you can load it on the truck, and then we need to backfill the grave."

As the machine operator began loading the box onto the flatbed, Darrel began to do a thorough examination of the grave hole as the State required, making sure nothing of the deceased was left behind before it was refilled.

Starting at the foot of the grave, he scanned along the walls and toward the headstone. Something stopped him, sending a chill up his backbone. Sticking out from the dirt was a hand, or rather the bones of a hand.

Surely that's not the dead guy's hand, is it?

He walked over to where the box was being set on the truck and signaled for the backhoe operator to stop. Ducking down, he searched the bottom of the box for any holes or cracks. There were none.

The funeral director stared at him, confused. "What are you doing?"

Darrel stood up. "Come here, I want to show you something."

5

LET'S PLAY

The big man followed Darrel over to the hole.

Darrel pointed. "What do you see?"

"Is that a...hand?"

"Yep, but there's no sign it could have come from the coffin we just exhumed."

"So, you think someone was buried under the existing grave?"

"I don't know, but do you have a ladder on your truck?"

"Sure. I'll be right back."

The funeral director hurried away, and when he returned, he was carrying a small stepladder. Darrel lowered it into the hole and climbed down into the grave. Taking a latex glove from his coat pocket, he brushed lightly at the exposed hand, mostly bone now. As he moved the dirt below the hand, it became clear there was an arm attached. He likely had a body.

Darrel climbed from the grave and pulled his phone out .

"Tell the backhoe guy to shut it off. I'm going to have to call this in before we go any further."

CHAPTER 1

Detective Jason Strong sat in the living room, bouncing his daughter Nina, now eighteen months old, on his knee. He was waiting for his wife to finish getting ready. It had become their morning routine to leave at the same time, whenever possible, thereby sharing the duties and pleasures of getting Nina ready for the babysitter.

Sandy came down the stairs with her blonde hair tied in a ponytail, wearing a pretty green blouse and black jeans. She smiled at the sight of her daughter giggling. "Are you having fun with Daddy?"

Jason stood, ending the ride, and handed Nina to her mommy. Walking over to the dining table, he picked up his phone, looking at a missed call. "I guess I'd better get going. That was Vanessa calling."

He kissed both of the ladies in his life and headed out the front door. Backing out of the driveway, he dialed his partner's

LET'S PLAY

number.

"This is Detective Layne."

"Vanessa, it's me."

"Morning, Jason. Are you on your way in?"

"Yeah; be there in ten minutes."

"That's fine, but I called to see if you wanted to meet me at a crime scene, rather than come all the way in."

"What have we got?"

"Lieutenant Banks got a call about a dead body at a cemetery."

Jason laughed. "Not this year, Vanessa! I remember April Fools from last year."

"That's what I thought when she told me, but this is for real."

"Oh, sure. What killed them? Too much time spent underground?"

It was Vanessa's turn to laugh. "Jason, I'm not kidding. We've got a body at a cemetery on the outskirts of the city."

Jason still wasn't buying it. "Okay, we better get over there and see what we can dig up!"

"Oh Jason, that was really bad."

"Can't blame a guy for trying. Look, I'll be in shortly, and then we can uncover the dirt on this case together." This time Jason laughed at his own joke.

"Fine. I'll be waiting for you in the

parking lot."

"Good. We need to get right on this grave situation."

The phone clicked in his ear.

"Vanessa?"

He folded his phone closed.

No one appreciates a good pun anymore.

****

Sure enough, when Jason pulled into the parking lot at the station, Vanessa was standing under the portico. Her blue eyes were hidden by sunglasses and her formerly long black hair now brushed the tops of her shoulders. Jason still hadn't got used to her in short hair, but Vanessa claimed her new look was much cooler in summer, which was fast approaching. He stopped in front of her and she climbed in. "Good morning, again."

"Good morning to you, too. You weren't kidding, were you?"

"Nope. A 'body at a cemetery' was what Banks gave me."

"Where?"

Vanessa glanced at her notes. "San Isidro Cemetery on Shepherd Road. Know it?"

LET'S PLAY

Jason shook his head. "Doesn't ring a bell."

"Take the 1604 Loop to Macdona Lacoste."

Jason pulled away from the curb and out into traffic. "You have any details?"

"Yeah. The call came in from Darrel Chase…"

"Doc's new assistant?"

"Yeah; he was officiating at an exhumation, and when they removed the coffin, he found another body in the dirt below."

"You're kidding."

"Nope."

"Why does he think it's a homicide?"

"He said the body didn't appear to be much older than six months, maybe less."

"That's wild."

She grinned at him. "Yeah, who'd think a body in a cemetery would be so weird."

****

San Isidro Cemetery was remote, with only a collection of cattle and horses as neighbors. When the two detectives pulled up at the front gate, they were met by the head of the Forensic Sciences Department,

Dr. Jocelyn Carter. Her brown hair was tucked up under a white skull cap, and the rest of her body was covered by a white cloth hazmat suit. Her black wired-framed glasses had been replaced by a similar pair of sunglasses.

"Hey Jason, Vanessa."

Jason looked past her into the hole that was now the hub of activity. "A personal appearance, Doc?"

She laughed. "Not by choice! Regulations say I've got to excavate these remains. We can't have you detectives just pulling them out the ground like dogs digging around in a garden, now can we?"

Jason put his hands up in front of him. "You won't catch me down in that hole."

Vanessa came up next to her partner. "Why not? Superstitious or just claustrophobic?"

"Neither, I just don't want to be underground until I have no choice."

"You mean when you're dead."

"Exactly, and even then I want to be cremated."

"So, it's worms you're afraid of?"

"Don't you worry about what I'm afraid of."

Doc Josie and Vanessa exchanged grins, rolling their eyes. Vanessa walked over to get a better look while Jason stayed

11

behind. "What have you learned so far, Doc?"

"The excavation is nearly half done. It appears to be the remains of a woman. She was buried with her jewelry on, and in what appears to be a pink bathrobe."

Jason nodded, watching two forensic techs dressed in the same suits as Doc Josie working around the body. Dirt was being brushed back from the remains, gathered into a bucket, and then lifted to the surface. Another tech was running the dirt through a portable sifter. Vanessa came back. "Come up with any ID?"

Doc Josie shook her head.

"What about cause of death?"

"Too soon to say for sure, but the skull does shows signs of trauma. I'll deliver the body to Doc Davis for an autopsy; DNA could help with identification."

Jason caught sight of Darrel Chase standing over by the backhoe and excused himself. The young coroner, in his mid-thirties, smiled when he recognized Jason.

"Detective Strong, how are you?"

"Hi, Doc. Call me Jason, please."

They shook hands.

"Okay Jason, call me Darrel."

Jason jabbed a thumb over his shoulder. "I gather you were the one who spotted the hand?"

12

"Yeah. It was sticking up through the dirt after we lifted the box."

"And it couldn't have come from the exhumed body?"

"Unlikely. I examined the coffin, and it was in pretty good shape. Besides, the body in the box is supposed to be a male."

Jason took out his pad. "Supposed to be?"

"Well, if it was me, I'd want to make sure the body in the coffin is who it's supposed to be."

Jason nodded. "Good thought. When was the coffin buried?"

"Last December."

"And you think the body is about the same age?"

"From a cursory exam, I'd say so."

Jason looked around over his shoulder. "Who's supposed to take the casket from here?"

"The funeral director over there. You want me to introduce you?"

"Please." Jason followed Darrel over to where a large man was trying to shade himself with the cab of the truck. Darrel introduced them.

"Jason, this is Terry Orman, he's the owner of Blessed Grace Funeral Home. Terry, this is Detective Jason Strong with SAPD Homicide."

13

LET'S PLAY

Jason shook his hand. "Terry, nice to meet you."

"What can I do for you, Detective?"

"You're supposed to take the coffin back to Blessed Grace?"

"Yes. The widow is waiting there now."

These kinds of things are very delicate, and Jason didn't want to be inconsiderate, but he liked Darrel's suggestion.

"Are you going to be moving the body to a new coffin?"

"Yes."

"I'd like to have a representative of the department there when you do that."

The funeral director thought about it, then shrugged. "I don't see where it would be a problem. Why?"

"Just for verification purposes." Jason turned to Darrel. "Do you mind taking care of that?"

A knowing look passed between the two men.

"Be glad to."

Jason turned back to funeral director. "Will you make sure that Dr. Chase gets notice when you're going to do the transfer?"

"Sure, no problem."

"Good. I'll talk to you later, Darrel."

Jason left the men standing there and

went back over to Vanessa, who stood watching Doc Josie and her team work.

She showed him her notepad. "I got the cemetery manager's number from the sign on the gate. Doc Josie said it will be awhile before their done. They're photographing everything in stages, and bagging anything that shows up in the sifter."

"Okay, why don't we call that number and see if we can get hold of the cemetery manager?"

"Works for me. Let's go."

****

Vanessa reached the manager of the San Isidro Cemetery on her first try.

"This is Detective Vanessa Layne with the SAPD. Can I ask who I'm speaking with?"

"Nathan Wolsey."

"Mr. Wolsey, I got this number off the sign at San Isidro. Are you the manager of the cemetery?"

"Yes, I run it for the cemetery board. What can I do for you?"

"My partner and I would like to speak with you. When could we do that?"

"How about now?"

15

LET'S PLAY

Vanessa gave Jason a thumbs up. "Great, where can we meet you?"

"Well, at the moment, I'm on a backhoe at the cemetery. Can you meet me there?"

Vanessa looked over her shoulder at the backhoe operator, just across from where they sat. Sure enough, he was on his cell phone. Vanessa looked at Jason and rolled her eyes. "That would be perfect; we'll see you in fifteen seconds."

She closed her phone and opened the car door. Jason was slow to catch on to what just happened. "Where are you going?"

"To interview the cemetery operations manager."

"You're going to walk?"

Vanessa shut the door and leaned back in through the window. "Yeah, unless you want to drive the two hundred feet over to the backhoe."

Jason laughed. "No, I think I can make it."

When they got over to Wolsey, he'd finished loading the coffin onto the bed of the funeral home's truck, and was gathering up his chains. He threw them into the digger's bucket before climbing up and shutting off the engine. Vanessa extended her hand as he jumped back to the ground. "Nathan Wolsey?"

16

"Yeah. Are you the detective who just called?"

"Yes, and this is my partner, Detective Strong."

"Nice to meet you. I gather your questions have to do with this exhumation."

Jason took out his notebook as Vanessa scanned the area. The funeral director was still tying the coffin to the truck bed, and Vanessa didn't want an audience for the interview.

"Mind if we go over by our car?"

Nathan shrugged. "Fine by me."

Jason led the way, Nathan behind him and Vanessa bringing up the rear. Vanessa guessed the young man to be in his late twenties, and he was thin enough that without his thick leather belt, his pants would probably slide to his ankles. His hair and skin were the same muddy brown, and whether it was from the dirt or natural color, Vanessa wasn't sure.

Jason leaned back against the front of their car, and Nathan imitated him, propping himself against the side fender. Vanessa stopped in front of the manager so she could look directly at him.

She smiled, trying to keep the young man relaxed. "How long have you been the manager here?"

"About nine months; I started last

17

June."

"And what do your duties include?"

"I mow, water, pick up the dead flowers, and do general maintenance like mending fences."

"Do you always do the digging?"

"Yes. The backhoe belongs to the cemetery board, and I run it whenever needed."

Vanessa's main interest was how the body might have gotten below the coffin. She pointed at the open hole currently filled with forensic techs. "Did you dig the original grave over there?"

"Yes. I dig the graves the night before the funeral and then backfill them after the funerals are over."

"Do you remember anything different about that grave?"

Nathan fidgeted slightly. "What do you mean by 'different'?"

"Oh, I don't know. Was the dirt disturbed? Did it look like someone may have been around the grave during the night?"

Nathan seemed to understand what Vanessa was getting at. "You mean did it look like someone had buried a body in it before the funeral?"

"That's an interesting theory, Nathan. Yeah, do think someone might have done that?"

Nathan cast a glance at Jason, looking for someone who wasn't quite so suspicious, but found no help. "You don't think I had anything to do with that body, do you?"

"Right now, we've just got a body, and we're not sure how it got there. Is it possible that you made a mistake and buried one over top of another?"

"No! I mean, I don't know how that could happen. I work from the map given me by the cemetery board. They tell me where to dig, and besides, I've never buried a body without a box."

The sweat running down the young man's face was making clean rivers through the dirt. They were standing in the shade, but it was warm. Vanessa couldn't decide if the sweat was from her questions or the heat.

"Can you give us the number to the cemetery board?"

"Sure, sure."

Nathan gave it from memory, and Jason wrote it down. He also recorded the name 'Elizabeth Fulton,' who Nathan said was the cemetery board president.

Vanessa decided she was finished for now. "Thanks for your help, Nathan. We'll be in touch."

The young man nodded and walked

19

back to his machine.

Jason gave Vanessa a smile. "Good work. You got him off balance nicely."

"Thank you, sir. I learned from the best."

"Very kind of you to say so."

"I was referring to Captain Patton."

Jason laughed. "You suck!"

Vanessa pointed at him as she got back in the car. "Got ya!"

JOHN C. DALGLISH

CHAPTER 2

The San Antonio River Walk was a winding trail, running from the Mission area on the south, to the San Antonio Zoo in the north. It was nearly fifteen linear miles of trail, used mostly by locals, except for the downtown section. What most visitors associated with the name River Walk was the section of the San Antonio River that looped off the main arm, over by The Alamo, and back again.

Restaurants, bars, tour boats, and shops all lined that area and attracted tourists year round. The last of the bars closed their doors at two in the morning, and the walk filled with a late-night rush of traffic, as partiers found their way to the vehicles that brought them. By then, cabs were lined up to bring people home, and the cleanup crew was busy emptying trashcans, riding motorized sweepers, and preparing the Walk for the next day's visitors.

LET'S PLAY

Jennifer Landers was one of the last to leave the RainTree Restaurant and Bar, partly because she'd stayed to talk to the cute guy in the surfer shorts, and partly because she couldn't find her girlfriend. The guy in the shorts was the same one Tammy-Jo was talking to the last time Jennifer saw her. He said he didn't know where Tammy-Jo went.

Being Tammy-Jo's ride back to the hotel, Jennifer didn't want to leave her friend behind. Several calls to Tammy's phone had gone to voicemail.

Jennifer walked carefully, swaying slightly, and checked each bench for her friend. It made sense Tammy-Jo would be waiting somewhere along the path to the car, but Jennifer was almost halfway to parking lot, and still no sign of her friend.

She spotted a worker emptying trashcans and wandered over, tapping him on the shoulder. "Hey."

The man, taller than Jennifer, wore a tan jumpsuit that zippered in front and bore the River Walk logo. He turned, startled by her approach from behind.

"Oh...hey yourself."

He looked to be in his late thirties, with shoulder length brown hair, and a beard already showing flecks of gray. His tone was friendly, but his eyes refused to meet hers.

22

Jennifer plopped down on the bench next to the garbage can he was emptying. "I'm looking for my friend and I wondered if maybe you saw her."

"There's a lot of people who come through here."

"Yeah, I know, but she's really cute. You would have noticed her."

"Really cute, huh?" He dropped the lid onto the can, a fresh bag inside. "Oh, well, that's different!"

He smiled, and realizing she was being teased, Jennifer giggled. She looked closely at the uniform and found his name. "Very funny, Anthony. I'm serious; I'm starting to get worried."

"Okay, I'm sorry. What does she look like?"

Jennifer rose unsteadily to her feet. "She's about the same height as me, has blonde shoulder length hair, and big green eyes. She was wearing a pink blouse with black jeans."

Anthony shook his head. "I'm sorry, but I don't think I've seen her."

Jennifer pouted. "What should I do now?"

"Well, you can report it to the police."

"I guess."

"Is it possible she got a ride with someone else?"

23

LET'S PLAY

"Yeah, I suppose."

"Maybe she's at home now."

"We're visiting."

"Oh, then maybe she's back at the hotel."

Jennifer was unconvinced. "Maybe. I guess I'll go there and check. Have a nice night, Anthony."

"You, too." He grabbed his trash cart and pushed it toward his next stop. "Be careful."

Jennifer, becoming increasingly wobbly, climbed the old stone steps on the west end of the River Walk, and crossed the road to where her car was parked. Hoping to find Tammy-Jo next to the car, she was disappointed to see no sign of her friend. Again, she tried the phone, and got the voicemail.

"Tammy-Jo, you better call me! I am so going to hurt you if you're ignoring my calls!"

She hung up, teetered in place awkwardly, and decided driving wasn't a good idea. Making her way over to where the taxis were lined up, she got in the one at the head of the line.

"Evening," the driver said in a raspy voice as he cranked over the fare meter. "Where to?"

"The Days Inn on East Houston Street,

please."

"You got it." The cab slowly pulled away from the curb.

Jennifer looked at the cabbie license, jammed into a clear plastic pocket hanging over the front seat in front of her. Ricardo Bonitez was thirty-nine, and had been driving a cab for two years. The picture could be better described as a mug shot, his round face covered with heavy stubble, and his thick eyebrows hanging over brown eyes.

"Have you been driving all night?"

His gaze flicked across to the rearview mirror, then back to the road. "Since seven this evening."

"I don't suppose you took another girl out to the Days Inn tonight, did you?"

He gave the question careful consideration before answering. "No...I haven't had any other fares in that direction."

Jennifer slumped back into the seat. "I didn't figure."

"Are you missing somebody?"

"Yeah. I'm not sure where my girlfriend is."

Bonitez leered into the rearview mirror. "Oh, you have a girlfriend, eh?"

Jennifer was caught by surprise, and instantly revolted. "No...No! She's my best

25

LET'S PLAY

friend, we're on vacation together."

"Oh, very sorry; I misunderstood."

Tammy-Jo had insisted on staying farther away from the River Walk to save money. Their room at the Days Inn was a third as much as a hotel downtown. It was only a ten-minute drive, but Jennifer suddenly couldn't wait to get out of the cab. As soon as they pulled up, she gave the driver a twenty and headed for her room. She didn't wait for change.

Still feeling the effects of the alcohol, she fumbled with the key for more than a minute before finally getting in. "Tammy-Jo?"

The room was empty. Jennifer checked the bathroom, and then flopped backward on the bed. "Tammy-Jo, where are you?"

For the umpteenth time, she tried her friend's cell phone. As it had before, it went to voicemail. She closed her phone, and without realizing it, her eyes. She was out cold in a flash.

****

Tammy-Jo Cousins screamed. Once, twice, and then a third time. "HELP!"

It was pointless. The sound bounced off the inside of the padded box and back at

26

her.

She punched at the lid, unable to straighten her arms to push, but it was solid. She only had a small beam of light, near her feet, from an air hole. The claustrophobic box brought on waves of nausea mixed with panic, and tears flowed down the sides of her face to the fabric beneath.

When she had first been put inside, naked from the waist down after being raped, there was a smell she couldn't identify. A strong, sickening, metallic odor. It finally dawned on her what it was; blood.

Not hers, she wasn't cut as far as she knew, but old blood. Dried blood. Someone else's blood.

Not knowing whoever or whatever left the blood, it served to trigger her brain that she might be the next to leave behind a similar stain. Paralyzing fear raked at her consciousness, as she struggled to push thoughts of how the blood got there out of her mind.

One of the first things her captor did, before driving to the house, was pull the battery out of her cell phone. Jennifer would be calling and getting no answer, and she hoped her friend was out there searching, but fear told Tammy-Jo she might be found too late.

She pleaded a silent message. *Please,*

27

LET'S PLAY

Jennifer, get help. Call the cops! Please!

The desperation of her own thoughts started a new wave of tears, and she closed her eyes, trying to shut out her insane reality.

****

The next morning, Jason and Vanessa arrived at the station at the same time, and rode the elevator to the third floor. Homicide took up the entire floor, but their desks were positioned only a few feet from the office of Lieutenant Sarah Banks, and they were always first on her radar. This morning, her door was closed and Jason wondered if the lieutenant was late again.

Banks had always been one to show up early for her shift, but a new boyfriend had changed priorities for her, and now she merely came in on time.

Jason was happy for Sarah, and even made light of it when it first happened.

"Alarm not working these days, Lieutenant?"

Her look froze Jason in place and sent Vanessa ducking behind the newspaper.

"Pardon?"

Jason had flipped open a file to hide

behind. "Nothing."

Banks laughed. "You chicken! My alarm works fine, I just didn't think I needed to be here so early to babysit you two."

Vanessa had poked her head up. "Right you are, Lieutenant. We can get to work without being told."

Banks had continued on to her office. "That's what I thought."

When she closed the door, Jason had dropped the file folder. "Brown-nose!"

Vanessa laughed. "Just because you stepped in it, doesn't mean I have to dive in after you."

He'd not made the same mistake since.

As the two detectives sat down, Jason's phone rang. "Detective Strong, Homicide."

"Jason, this is Doc Josie."

"Hey, Doc. What's up?"

"Have you got a minute?"

"Sure."

"Come on down here then, will ya?"

"Okay, see you shortly."

****

Jason and Vanessa rode the elevator to the basement, turning right as they exited,

29

and pushing through the glass doors leading to the Forensic Science Department. Doc Josie was waiting in her office and waved at them. "In here."

Jason took a chair in front of the doc while Vanessa chose to stand in the doorway. Doc Josie looked up at the female detective. "Do you mind coming in and shutting the door?"

Though surprised, Vanessa complied with the request. She leaned back against the closed door.

The doc would usually greet them with a smile, but it was missing this morning, as she opened the file sitting on the desk in front of her.

"I've got an ID on the remains from San Isidro. You're not going to believe it."

She slid a photo across the desk as Vanessa took a seat next to Jason. Doc Josie waited while the detectives studied the photo. Vanessa was the first to realize it.

"Is that...?"

Doc nodded. "I matched the dental records this morning."

Jason looked from one woman to the other. "Am I missing something?"

Doc slid a second photo in front of Jason, this one from a missing persons poster. Jason looked up at Josie. "Really?"

"Really; Melinda Gomez. She was the

first girl associated with the River Walk Missing."

Jason picked up the poster and scanned the information. Melinda Gomez was a pretty twenty-three-year-old, with short brown hair and brown eyes, who had gone missing six months ago. Last seen around closing time on Saturday, December 16, she'd been visiting from Houston and never returned to her hotel room.

"How many have gone missing now?"

"Three. None had been found until now."

"Do we have a cause of death?"

"I believe Doc Davis is just finishing the autopsy, so you might get to see some of it."

Vanessa snorted. "Oh, goody!"

Doc Josie laughed, then immediately turned serious again. "I've made Captain Patton aware of what I just told you. He wants a tight rein on information and only those who need to know are to be told for now. The Missing are an extremely sensitive subject."

Vanessa stood up. "Politically?"

"Yes, and economically."

Jason was surprised. "You don't usually get involved in that kind of stuff, Doc."

"I know, but the order for discretion

31

LET'S PLAY

had come down several months ago.
Anything tied to the Missing needed to be
run directly up the chain to the captain first."

Vanessa refused to hide her cynicism.
"Yeah, because we don't want any news
getting out that would hurt tourism, even if
the families could have closure."

"You're preaching to the choir,
Vanessa," Doc closed the folder and handed
it to Jason. "Nonetheless, I'd prefer to keep
my job."

Jason passed the folder to his partner.
"Me too."

"Whatever." Vanessa scowled, and
then laughed. "Me too."

They left the office and went directly
across the hall to the den of the Medical
Examiner. They found Doc Davis hunched
over a table, a lighted magnifying lens in
front of his face, peering down into the skull
on the table. The big man was past
retirement age but showed no signs of
slowing down. Jason was sure the doc could
out-work his new assistant despite being
nearly three decades older.

"Hey, Doc."

He didn't look up from his studying.
"Hi, Jason. Layne with you?"

Vanessa laughed. "Yup, Layne's with
him."

"Good, you two come over here."

32

Jason and Vanessa exchanged looks, but did as they were asked. Jason led the way. "What you got, Doc?"

Doc Davis leaned back, away from the magnifier which sat poised over a skull, now cleaned of all remaining flesh. "Look through there."

Jason did. "What am I looking at?"

Doc didn't answer. "You too, Vanessa."

Jason backed up and was replaced by Vanessa. She looked, then stood up quickly. "Same question as Jason. What are we looking at?"

"Cause of death for the victim. It appears to be a blow from the head of a hammer."

Jason looked again. "How can you tell?"

"See the round impact location?"

"Yeah."

"And the symmetrical fracturing around the hole that leads away from the wound?"

Jason stood up. "Yeah."

"That's consistent with a round blunt object, like a hammer head, delivered with a large amount of force. That means a murder, not an accident, was covered up by the burial."

"What about the cause of death? Can

33

you tell if the victim was alive when she was buried?"

Doc Davis stripped off his gloves and washed his hands at the sink next to the body. He was shaking his head. "There wasn't enough lung tissue left to tell if she inhaled dirt or not."

Vanessa shuddered and Jason figured she was thinking the same thing as him.

I hope she wasn't buried alive.

CHAPTER 3

Jennifer approached the front desk of the San Antonio police station, her nervousness outweighed by her worry. Tammy-Jo had not come back to the hotel that morning, and calls to her phone still went unanswered. Jennifer had no doubt her friend was in trouble.

"Excuse me."

An officer turned around. He was short with gray hair and kind eyes, and his badge identified him as Sergeant Connor. "Can I help you?"

"I hope so. I need to report a missing person."

"I see." The sergeant sat down and drew a paper from the stack to his right. "Who is the person you're reporting?"

"My friend, Tammy-Jo Cousins."

"How long has she been missing?"

"I haven't seen or heard from her since last night."

LET'S PLAY

"How old is she?"

"Twenty-two."

Sergeant Connor looked up at her. "We normally don't consider someone missing after just twelve hours."

"But she is missing! I know it." Tears started down her cheeks and the officer seemed anxious to comfort her. "It's okay. Do you think your friend is in trouble?"

Jennifer struggled to control herself. "Yes."

"Why?"

"We're here on vacation, just the two of us, and she wouldn't have left me alone without talking to me."

The sergeant seemed to pause, as if deciding what to do next. "Where did you last see your friend?"

"At the RainTree Restaurant."

"Which one? There's a couple here in the city."

"The one on the River Walk."

Without another word, the sergeant picked up a phone and pushed several buttons. While he waited for an answer, he pointed at a bench across the hall. "If you'll sit over there, I'll get someone to take your report."

"Okay. Thank you."

Less than five minutes went by before someone came looking for her.

36

****

Detective Eli Warren hung up the phone, quickly fixed his blue tie, checked to make sure his white shirt was tucked in, and headed for the lobby. Taking the stairs two at a time down from the second floor, he came out into the main foyer huffing from the exertion, and marched over to Dave Connor.

"Where is she, Dave?"

The old sergeant handed the report he'd started to the detective and pointed at the bench across the hall. Eli strode over to the petite dark-haired girl, forcing himself to smile despite being winded.

"My name is Detective Warren. You said your friend is missing?"

"Yes. Her name is Tammy-Jo Cousins."

"What's your name?"

"Jennifer Landers."

"Nice to meet you, Jennifer. Where did you say you last saw Miss Cousins?"

"At the RainTree Bar on the River Walk."

"Okay Jennifer, would you come with me?"

She stood. "Of course."

37

LET'S PLAY

Eli pushed the button for the elevator and the two rode up to the second floor in silence. He ran his hand repeatedly through a mop of red hair, the nervous habit he developed in the academy. When the doors opened, he guided her to his desk, and offered her a seat. "Would you like anything to drink?"

"No, thanks."

The detective moved his bulky frame around to the other side and sat down. When he looked up, the girl was staring at some pictures pinned on the bulletin board next to his desk. They were the information posters on the three missing River Walk girls. She looked back at him, fear evident in her eyes.

"I saw one of those photos at the bar. Do you think the same person took my friend?"

"No, at least I hope not. Let's get the facts first before we jump to conclusions, okay?"

He smiled and she nodded, but the fear he'd seen in her eyes didn't subside.

"I have your friend's name and age. Where is she from?"

"We're on vacation from Lincoln. We're sophomores at the University of Nebraska."

"And the last time you saw Tammy-Jo, what was she doing?"

38

"She was dancing with a guy."

"Do you know what his name was?"

"Denny...Kenny. I'm not sure. I talked to him before I left, but he said he didn't know where Tammy-Jo went after they danced."

"Do you think you could describe this guy?"

"Sure. He was maybe six-two, sandy brown hair, wore an Ocean Pacific t-shirt and surfer shorts."

Eli had not come across a similar description in the witness reports of the other three girls. "Would you mind giving a more in-depth description to one of our sketch artists?"

"Sure, if it'll help."

The detective placed the call requesting a sketch artist before continuing. When he turned back to Jennifer, she was staring at the posters again. "Now Jennifer, I need you to give me a description of Tammy-Jo."

"Oh, I have something better; a picture." She fished the photo out of her purse and handed it to the detective. Eli examined it, silently hoping the face looking back at him wasn't going to be the next poster pinned to his wall. "What about her clothes? What was she wearing last night?"

"She was wearing a pink blouse with

39

black jeans and pink flip-flops."

"Okay. What about jewelry or a purse?"

"She always wears a red rubber bracelet that says 'Huskers Rule.' It's from our school's football games. Her purse was a black leather clutch."

"What about family?"

"She's an only child. Her parents are on vacation somewhere. Tammy-Jo didn't mention where, but I have their number."

"Good."

Eli finished his report just as Captain Patton stepped out of the elevator.

****

After visiting Doc Davis, Jason and Vanessa headed upstairs to the second floor. When the elevator doors opened, they found a dark-haired girl sitting with a sketch artist at Eli Warren's desk. Jason recognized the artist from a previous case.

"Hey, George. How ya doin'?"

George Stewart, the epitome of the word 'geek,' looked up from thick tortoise-shell glasses. He'd been the sketch artist at SAPD for more than two decades.

"Hey, Jason."

"Do you know where Eli is?"

The artist pointed his pencil behind him. "In the conference room with Patton."

"Okay, thanks."

Jason, with Vanessa right behind him, went over and knocked on the conference room door. After a minute, the captain opened it. He looked them up and down once, then swung the door wide. "Good timing. You two, come in here."

They nodded at Eli and took seats around a square table while the captain looked at a file folder. The conference room was smaller than the one in Homicide but just as poorly lit. When Patton looked up, he was clearly troubled.

"I just filled in Eli on what Doc Josie found this morning. Right now, you three, Docs Davis and Josie, the Chief, and I are the only ones who know the identity of our victim. Chief Murray is going to see the mayor. We want this to stay out of the papers as long as possible."

Vanessa shifted uncomfortably in her chair. "What about the family?"

"They'll be told soon, and asked to keep it private for the time being."

"Won't they want to have a funeral?"

"I'm sure, but the body won't be released while the investigation is still going on anyway."

Jason looked over at Eli. "What's

41

LET'S PLAY

George Stewart doing up here?"

Eli looked weary, his dark eyes bloodshot and his curly black hair showing tinges of gray that Jason didn't remember. His dark skin was pale and drawn.

"You saw the girl sitting at my desk?"

Jason nodded.

"She came in this morning to report her friend missing."

Jason could see in the detective's face what he'd left unsaid. "River Walk?"

Eli nodded and Vanessa groaned.

Patton let his gaze move from one detective to the next in the silent room.

"If our first victim is reported deceased, then it's likely the press and the public will jump to the conclusion that all three of the others are also dead. While we know that's a possibility, we are still looking at the other two cases, as well as the new one, as missing persons."

Jason leaned forward in his chair. "We have to treat them as connected though."

"Yes, and the first thing you two are going to do is review all of Eli's files. There has to be something besides the abduction site to connect the cases, and fresh eyes won't hurt. Eli is going to pursue the new case on its own merits."

Jason tipped his head toward the closed door. "Who is Stewart sketching?

The missing girl?"

"No, we have a photo of her." Patton slid it across the desk for Jason and Vanessa to look at. "The sketch is of the last man seen talking to the missing girl."

"Okay, we'll need a copy of that."

"Done. The forensic and autopsy reports will land on my desk first, then be passed on to the three of you."

Jason turned to Eli. "Can you order the phone records for the new case?"

"Sure. I'll do it as soon as we're done here."

"Where are the files on your investigations?"

"The bulk of them are in Records. All three of my cases had gone cold, that is until this morning."

Jason and Vanessa exchanged glances and then looked at the captain. Patton gave them the signal. "Off you go, and report only to me."

Vanessa's eyebrows shot up. "What about Lieutenant Banks?"

"I'll speak to her and let you know when she's been brought into the loop."

The two detectives stood and left the room. On the elevator to the basement, Vanessa couldn't hide her annoyance. "Why do you think the whole thing is so hush-hush?"

43

LET'S PLAY

"Trying to keep people calm, maybe?"

He doubted that was the real reason and Vanessa wasn't buying it either.

"We both know what the River Walk means to this city. I think I smell the odor of a Chamber of Commerce panic."

Jason smiled. "Maybe."

The elevator doors opened and they took the long hallway directly in front of them. The Records Department was overseen by one Marie Turley. She'd been with the department nearly forty years and her memory was legendary.

She was one of Jason's favorite people and he always looked forward to seeing her. When they came through the entrance, Marie had her back to the detectives. "Be with you in a moment."

Jason winked at Vanessa. "We don't have all day, you know!"

Jason could see the clerk's back stiffen slightly, before she turned around slowly. "Well, that's a problem, because with that attitude, it may take all day."

Jason stood grinning at her and Marie's face cracked wide with a smile. "Jason! I didn't know it was you. Come here and give me a hug, you dog."

Marie came around the counter and Jason hugged her like she was his mother. "Good to see you, Marie."

Vanessa was treated to a hug of her own. "Hi, Marie."

The records clerk went back to her side of the counter. "What brings you two down here?"

Jason laughed. "Just needed a hug, that's all."

Marie grinned. "Anytime!"

"Actually, we need the three files on the River Walk Missing."

"Really? Something new come up?"

"This is a military case, I'm afraid, Marie."

"Oh, I see. Don't ask, don't tell."

Jason nodded. Marie turned to go into the expanse of shelves that disappeared into the far reaches of the basement. "It'll take some time to gather it all; you want me to send them up to the third floor?"

"Perfect."

"Okay, talk to you later."

LET'S PLAY

CHAPTER 4

Footsteps echoed through the box as they came closer to where she lay. She wasn't cold, but a shiver ran down Tammy-Jo's spine anyway, and fear battled with hope that someone other than her captor was coming. The lid opened, blinding her temporarily, but when her eyes adjusted, she was again looking at her nightmare.

"Time to come out and play."

She started to cry, wiping at her eyes with her sleeve, until she suddenly remembered she was naked from the waist down. Sitting up, she pulled at her shirt, trying to stretch it over her thighs.

"Please…let me go. I won't tell anybody. I don't even know where we are."

His voice was friendly, almost warm, and it sent chills through her. "You wouldn't want to leave yet. We're going to get to know each other a little better while we watch our favorite show."

"Our show...what show?" Tammy-Jo's brain spun, unable to make sense of his words. "I don't even know you."

He appeared not to hear her. "Go into the bathroom and change. There's a pink bathrobe laying folded on the counter; put it on. Leave the rest of your clothes in the bathroom."

Tammy-Jo looked in the direction he was pointing. At the end of the hall was a door, sitting slightly ajar, with a light on. Adrenaline surged through her.

That could be my way out.

Moving slowly toward the bathroom, she kept her eyes to the floor, feeling his stare as she walked.

"Hurry up; our dinner is almost ready."

When she reached the bathroom, Tammy-Jo darted inside and closed the door behind her. The lock on the doorknob had been removed. She spun around, searching for a window, and her heart sank. The window had iron bars across it and was boarded up on the other side.

Next, she searched her surroundings for a weapon. Pulling back the shower curtain revealed an empty tub, without so much as a bar of soap. There was no hairbrush, toothbrush, or other implement on the countertop. Pulling the vanity cabinet doors open, she found an empty space. Then

47

it dawned on her that there wasn't even a mirror to break for a glass shard.

She dropped down on the toilet, whose lid and tank cover had been removed, and stared at the pink robe folded next to her. She couldn't fathom what sick reason he had for wanting her in that, and the thought of his hands on her again caused her to vomit.

THUMP! THUMP! THUMP!

Tammy-Jo rocketed straight to her feet at the pounding on the door, her heart in her throat.

"Hurry up in there!"

She forced herself to take a deep breath. "Uh…okay; be out in a minute."

Unable to see any escape and not wanting to get him any angrier, she removed her blouse and bra, and put on the robe. Wrapping it as tight as she could, she tied the sash in a double knot. When she opened the door, he was at the far end of the hall waiting for her.

He appeared to be in the same clothes as last night, but now wore a brown belt with a leather sheath hanging from it. Protruding from the sheath was the carved-bone handle of the knife he'd used to kidnap her the previous night.

"You look nice. Now come eat before dinner gets cold."

As she moved toward him, she

48

checked her surroundings. One door came
up on her left and another on her right. Both
were closed, as was a third door straight
ahead. That was the room she'd come from.
She figured the windows in the other rooms
would be barred and boarded as well.

Following him around the corner, she
came into the living room, which she'd seen
on the way in. Tammy-Jo wasn't old enough
to know what a house in the nineteen-
seventies looked like, but she guessed this
would be it. In the kitchen beyond, she saw
a gold fridge, a stove the same color, and a
green sink inside a yellow countertop. The
sink overflowed with dishes and the stove
had a skillet on it.

The television was off, but sitting
directly in front of it were two orange velour
chairs, and matching portable dinner trays
with gold folding legs. A plate had been set
on each.

"Sit."

She started to take the nearest chair,
but he stopped her. "Not that one!" The
anger in his voice made her jump. "The one
on the left."

Tammy-Jo scooted around the food
tray and dropped into the well-worn chair.
The robe fell open at her thighs and she
quickly closed it. He pretended not to notice
as he sat down next to her, then pointed a

49

LET'S PLAY

remote at TV.

It came to life with an episode from the long-running series *Two and a half men* on. "Oh good, this is one of my favorites."

She sat stiffly, staring at the food on the plate in front of her, but afraid to touch it. He began to eat, then smiled at her. "Go ahead, I'm sure you're hungry."

She was, and despite her fear, she attacked what turned out to be some type of Goulash. She stuffed huge forkfuls into her mouth, and then washed them down with the glass of water next to the plate. When she paused from her eating, Tammy-Jo realized he wasn't paying any attention to her. Instead, he was eating and occasionally laughing at the show.

She studied him while trying not to be obvious. She remembered now where she'd met him and cursed herself for not being smarter. He'd looked harmless at the time, and still did as he sat there watching TV, but she'd seen the angry side of him last night. She didn't want to provoke him.

With just a little left on her plate, it dawned on her she didn't know what was going to happen after the food, and chastised herself for not eating slower. She began taking small bites while scanning the room. When she finished the last one, her need for a cigarette forced her to speak.

"Can I have a smoke?"

He turned quickly, his fierce look taking her by surprise. "No, it makes you stink. Don't ask again."

Just as quickly, the look vanished and he returned to his TV watching. She returned to checking her surroundings.

The living room continued the seventies theme. A black velvet painting of Elvis Presley hung behind the TV, long gold tassels dangled from the drapes, and a pair of table lamps had green shades with even more tassels.

An old photo, hanging over the doorway to the kitchen, froze her in place and caught the breath in her throat. A slightly younger version of her captor was sitting at a tray table and watching TV. Next to him, a smiling girl about the same age as him ate at a matching tray table. The girl was wearing a pink bathrobe.

Tammy-Jo retched, nearly throwing her dinner up all over the robe. She began to shake and her captor stopped chewing in mid-bite. "Are you okay?"

She nodded, but kept a hand over her mouth, as she tried to quell the panic rising inside.

****

51

LET'S PLAY

Jason was on his way home when his phone rang.

"Hello?"

"Jason, this is Darrel Chase."

Jason looked at his watch. "You're working late."

"Yeah, a little. I wanted to let you know I attended the opening of the coffin over at Blessed Grace."

"Good. What did you find?"

"He was who he was supposed to be. Jacob Samuel Moore."

"Okay Darrel, thanks. At least that's one possibility we can cross off."

"Anytime, Jason. Good night."

Jason hung up as he pulled into his driveway. As he always did, Jason made a conscious effort to close off the work of the day and focus on his family. When a young girl is missing and three others may already be dead, it's tough to do. Still, he owed it to Sandy and Nina.

He sucked in a deep breath and let out a sigh. Opening the car door, he spied a tiny face looking at him through the front window. The sight of his precious daughter did more to wash away the day than any effort on his part.

****

Tammy-Jo laid in the closed box, apparently relocked for the night, with dried tears staining her face. They had watched a second episode of the sitcom before he took their plates to the kitchen. When he returned, he told her to fold the bathrobe up in the bathroom, and come to bed.

She'd sat unmoving, sobs causing her body to vibrate. When she didn't comply, he'd reached down, grabbed her by the arm, and dragged her down the hallway. Once in the bathroom, he pulled the robe off her.

"Now fold it."

He stood watching while she tried to fold it the same way she'd found it. When her re-fold had been found to be lacking, he'd cussed at her, grabbed the robe, and threw it on the floor.

"Do it again and this time do it right!"

She had folded it more carefully the second time, as he watched with his hand resting on the knife. When she was done, he'd forced her into his bedroom, next to where her box was kept. This time he'd raped her twice.

Now naked and cold, she laid still, hoping he was done for the night.

LET'S PLAY

The next morning, Jason and Vanessa found Marie had delivered several boxes to each of their desks. In addition, there were three more on the floor by Jason's desk. Jason looked at the boxes and then to Vanessa. "Conference room?"

"Conference room it is."

Together they moved all the files into the conference room and started sorting through them. They'd been at it an hour and a half before Jason realized he hadn't had any coffee.

"Time out!"

He made the 'T' with his hands and stood up. Vanessa laughed. "Okay. What's up?"

"Coffee. I need some."

"Sounds good. I'll take some, too."

Jason left the room to get two cups of coffee. When he returned, Vanessa had a tape in the video machine and was watching some surveillance replays. He passed her a cup and sat down next to her.

"What are you looking at?"

"I found the city's closed-circuit recordings of the River Walk."

Jason squinted at the grainy black-and-white images. "Pause it a sec."

54

Vanessa did and Jason closed the blinds as well as shut off the lights. "That's better. Go ahead."

Vanessa restarted the video. "This is from the night Melinda Gomez went missing. It's been reviewed, of course, but I figured we would want our own look."

It took a few minutes to spot their girl for the first time, but after that, she was easy to follow. She came out of the RainTree Bar alone, turned and waved her cup at someone still inside, and then walked unsteadily toward the west end of the River Walk. Whoever had been in the bar didn't follow her.

In fact, it wasn't until she threw her plastic cup away that she had any interactions at all. The River Walk employee standing next to the trash can looked as though he tried to engage her in conversation, but she wandered off seemingly without speaking to him. He didn't follow her.

The last place she appeared on the video was at the taxi stand, where she gets into the back of a cab. Jason already knew she never made it back to her hotel. He flipped open the book of interviews he'd retrieved from Melinda's file.

"I see an interview with the River Walk employee and another with the cabbie,

LET'S PLAY

but no reference to the person or persons she waved at in the bar."

"What did the Walk employee have to say?"

"He said he remembered speaking to her, but denied seeing her after that. He took a polygraph but the results were inconclusive."

"What about the cab driver?"

"He said it was a long night but he thought he remembered her. He claimed to have dropped her off at her hotel."

"Did he take a poly?"

"Yes, same result as the employee. He also provided a copy of his log book."

Jason's phone began to ring. "This is Strong."

"Yes, Detective Strong, this is Elizabeth Fulton with the Bexar County Rural Cemetery Association. I'm returning your call."

Her all-business tone subconsciously prompted Jason sit up straighter in his chair. "Yes, Miss Fulton…"

"It's Mrs. Fulton."

"Mrs. Fulton…I apologize. What I called in reference to was the exhumation the other day at San Isidro."

"Yes, I heard about that. Shocking."

"Indeed. Have you ever had something like that happen at San Isidro before?"

Her indignation came through clearly. "Detective Strong, I assure you that something like this would never happen under normal circumstances."

"Do you have any idea how it did occur then?"

"I certainly do not and I would think that is something for you to be looking into. We have procedures in place to prevent such things from happening at any of our cemeteries."

"I'm sorry, did you say any?"

"Yes, why?"

"How many cemeteries does the board oversee?"

"Currently, there are six."

That explained why such a small cemetery had its own backhoe.

"Mrs. Fulton, you have an employee who does your maintenance..."

"Yes, Nathan Wolsey."

"Does he perform the same duties at all six of the cemeteries?"

"Yes."

"Including digging graves for funerals?"

"Yes, of course. Why do you ask?"

"Just gathering general information. Can you give me a list of your other cemeteries?"

"Sure."

57

Jason wrote them down as Elizabeth Fulton named them. "Thank you, ma'am. Do you know where Nathan is working today?"

"I believe he's doing fence repair at San Isidro. Will that be all, Detective?"

"Yes, for now. Thank you for calling.

Jason hung up and looked at his partner. "Remember Mr. Wolsey?"

"Of course."

"He has five other cemeteries where he does the digging."

"Really?" Vanessa shut off the video. "I think we need to go speak to our friend Mr. Wolsey."

"I agree, but let's stop at Stumpy's first."

"Ooooh, that sounds good."

"Any food sounds good to you!"

****

They beat the lunch rush and took a table near the window as usual. Their food came quickly and as they sat finishing, they were surprised by a visitor to their table.

"Good afternoon, Detectives."

Jason and Vanessa looked up to see Devin James, the senior city reporter from the San Antonio News. Vanessa went back to her lunch, but Jason smiled up at him. "Hey, Devin."

"Mind if I pull up a chair?" He didn't wait for an answer, sitting down at the same time he asked.

"Suit yourself."

"So Jason, I heard something interesting, and you're just the person to verify it."

Jason studied the face of the reporter. Devin's eyes were always bright against his dark skin, but today they seemed to have an extra glint, and that could only mean trouble. "I doubt it."

Devin ignored his tone, plunging ahead.

"It has been suggested to me that you found the body of Melinda Gomez, one of the River Walk Missing."

Both Jason and Vanessa stopped mid-chew and stared at James. The reporter grinned, obviously pleased with his surprise. "It appears my information is good."

Jason set down his fork. "Where did you hear that?"

"Oh come on, Jason, you know I can't tell you that."

"I'm not going to verify that, James."

"Okay, but maybe you could tell me if there's a suspect that has come to the forefront based on the discovery."

59

"No comment."

"Can you tell me how the discovery was made?"

"No comment."

"What about cause of death?"

"Devin, please excuse yourself from our table. We would like to finish our lunch in peace."

Devin looked at Vanessa, who still had her head down, then at Jason. Their eyes met for a long moment before James stood. "Enjoy your lunch, Detectives."

Jason watched the reporter walk away, then looked at Vanessa. "Crap!"

****

An hour later, the two detectives parked at the entrance gate to San Isidro Cemetery. They found Nathan Wolsey working on the fence near the back of the property. He didn't appear happy to see them. "Detectives, what brings you out here?"

Jason took out his notepad as Vanessa took the lead with the manager, as she had the last time. "We had a few more questions."

"You could have called."

"It's so peaceful here; we thought it

would be nice to visit in person."

Nathan dropped the pliers he was using into a toolbox on the ground. "So what is it you needed?"

"When we spoke the other day, you failed to mention your other duties."

"What?"

"Your other duties."

"I'm not sure what you mean."

"Isn't it true that you are the manager and groundskeeper for six cemeteries?"

"Well, sure, but...I didn't think that mattered."

Vanessa pressed him. "It does matter, Nathan. In fact, it matters a lot. You dig the graves at all six, correct?"

"Yeah, so what?"

"Did you notice anything unusual about any of those graves in the last six months?"

The young man was sweating profusely, and not from the heat. The day was cooler than the previous several, and a nice breeze ruffled their shirts. "What do you mean?"

"Think, Nathan. Disturbed dirt, graves that seemed altered, things out of place from the way you left them the night before."

"I don't know. I can't remember any."

"What about last December, on the sixteenth, would you be able to tell us where you were that day?"

"Six months ago! I doubt it. Hey, what is this about? Are you trying to say I was responsible for the body we found the other day?"

Jason stepped forward, laying his hand on the young man's shoulder. "We're not saying anything right now, Nathan. We just want to make sure we have all the facts, and it's disturbing you withheld information from us."

"I didn't withhold...I'm sorry... I didn't think it was important."

Jason handed Nathan his card. "Okay. If you think of anything else, you be sure and let us know, okay?"

"Yeah...of course."

"Great. We'll let you get back to work now."

Jason and Vanessa headed back to their car. Jason put away his notepad. "What do you think?"

"The kid gets very nervous, doesn't he?"

"Yeah, I think we should run a criminal history on him. In the meantime, we have to meet with the captain. He's gonna want to know about what James said."

"He's not going to be happy, that's for sure."

Jason opened his car door and looked across the hood at Vanessa. "I'm clean. You?"

"I'm clean, but still, I hate being the bearer of bad news."

They climbed in and Jason started the vehicle. "Me, too."

He took out his phone and called Patton's office. In a short conversation with Mary, they made an appointment for three o'clock.

LET'S PLAY

CHAPTER 5

Mary Faldo smiled at the detectives when they came into the office.

"Go on in, he's expecting you."

Jason held the door for Vanessa. "After you, madam."

She rolled her eyes. "James is your buddy, I'm not telling the captain."

Jason smiled at being caught. "Okay, okay."

John Patton rose from behind his desk and shook hands with his detectives. "Good to see you both, I think. Why the meeting?"

The captain hadn't lost any of the muscle he'd worked so hard to get while in charge of Homicide. "You're looking good, John."

His friend's bushy eyebrows went up. "Oh, no. Small talk, that's bad."

Jason laughed and took the seat offered to him. Vanessa stayed standing. Jason got right to the point.

"Devin James stopped by our table at lunch today."

"Another bad sign."

This time Vanessa laughed. "You have no idea."

Jason gave her a dirty look. "Anyway, he said someone had given him an interesting piece of information."

"About what?"

"It seems he was informed we had discovered the body of Melinda Gomez."

The captain studied his detective with a blank face. Finally, he looked at Vanessa, then back at Jason. "I trust I can rule you two out as the source of this information?"

"It wasn't us, John."

Patton leaned forward and picked up his phone. "Mary?"

He listened, and then. "Get me Chief Murray, please."

He put the phone down and waited, still watching his detectives in silence. Jason decided keeping his mouth shut right now was the wisest option. The phone buzzed and Patton picked it up.

"Bill, this John. I have Strong and Layne in with me. You got a minute?"

The captain nodded. "We'll wait."

He hung up and looked at Jason. "Tell me how it went."

"He said he been told we found the

65

body. He asked for verification and I said 'no comment.' Our reaction probably told him what he needed."

"He caught you by surprise."

"You could say that."

"What else?"

"He wanted COD and any information I could give him on suspects. I stuck with the no comment spiel and asked him to leave us alone."

Patton nodded as the door to his office opened. Chief Murray, wearing his standard tie, white shirt with dark slacks, and boyish haircut, came into the room, nodding at both detectives.

He turned to Patton. "What's up?"

The captain filled his boss in, and when he was done, the chief stared out the window. "You two are sure you weren't the source?"

They answered in unison. "We're sure."

"Who else knew, John?"

"Davis, the new guy Chase, Doc Josie, Eli Warren, and Lieutenant Banks. I filled her in this morning."

"Okay, I want you to speak to each of them personally. No phone calls. I'll check my end with the mayor's office."

The captain nodded.

Murray directed his attention toward

JOHN C. DALGLISH

the two detectives. "What have we got on
the case to this point?"

Jason had brought the sketch from
Jennifer Landers and handed it to the chief.
"That sketch is from number four's best
friend, he's the last person she saw her
friend talking to, but we don't have an ID on
the guy yet. We also have two names we're
looking into from the original file, and one
we've discovered ourselves."

"Anything promising?"

"Not yet, Chief."

"Okay, stay on it, and keep the captain
up to date."

"Yes, sir."

Their presence no longer required, the
two detectives beat a hasty retreat. On the
elevator down to the third floor, Jason let
out a sigh. "That was fun."

"Yeah. Hanging out with you, Strong,
is a kick!"

He laughed. "Thanks!"

****

It was still daylight when he unlocked
the box the next time. The glow blinding her
wasn't just the overhead bulb, but the
sunlight hitting a living room window,
which was streaming through the bedroom

67

LET'S PLAY

door.

"Time to play."

In one hand, he was holding the pink bathrobe out to her, while the other rested on the hilt of the knife. Struggling to stand, she grasped at the robe and pulled herself up. As quickly as she could, she wrapped the robe around her. Next, he handed her a hairbrush, and pointed toward a mirror hung on the wall.

"You may feel better if you brush your hair."

She took the brush, knowing instantly it was too small to be an effective weapon, and walked to the mirror. She was horrified, but not surprised, at her reflection. Her blonde hair was tangled and matted, her eyes sunken, and her skin pale.

Pulling the brush through her hair, she did her best to make herself feel human again; a nearly impossible task with that animal watching her. Eventually, she handed the brush back and followed him out to the living room. There was a card table set up, a pitcher and two glasses sitting on it.

"You sit over there."

She went to the chair he indicated, her body propelled by a kind of nightmarish autopilot, and sat with her hands in her lap. He poured her a drink and then one for himself. Thirst drove her to grab the glass

68

and guzzle it, her brain registering the flavor of peach iced tea as it went down.

He sat opposite her and sipped his own, watching her over the rim of his glass. "More?"

Tammy-Jo nodded slightly, putting her glass down. He refilled it and this time she drank it more slowly.

"Dinner is frozen pizza, and I'll put it in the oven soon, but I thought we could play some cards first."

"What kind of cards?" Her voice sounded unfamiliar; distant, lifeless.

"Do you know how to play Gin Rummy?"

She nodded.

"Good. We'll play a few hands before dinner."

He reached behind him, picked up a deck of cards, shuffled them, and dealt seven each. Tammy-Jo looked at the greasy playing cards but didn't move. He was busy fixing his hand when he noticed. "Go ahead, pick them up."

It wasn't a request, or at least it didn't feel like one to her, and she slowly picked up one card at a time. He resumed fixing his hand and when he was done, he looked up at her.

"You're first."

LET'S PLAY

Jason was on his way home when his phone began to ring. It was next to him on the seat, and he recognized the number as he picked it up.

"What is it, James?"

"Jason, why so formal? After all, I was calling you as a favor."

"Really? Well, forgive me for being so rude!"

"You really are a cynic, Strong, you know that?"

"Funny, no one else ever tells me that; maybe it's just you."

Devin allowed himself a chuckle. "I'm calling with a heads-up."

"To what?"

"The body found at San Isidro is going to be front page in the morning."

Jason didn't respond, instead trying to picture the look on the captain's face when he heard about it.

"Jason?"

"Yeah?"

"This is your chance to check any details you might want to make sure are correct."

"Still no comment."

"Okay."

Jason was about to hang up, but he knew Devin had done him a favor. "I gotta go, but James…"

"Yeah?"

"Thanks."

"Don't mention it." The phone clicked and Jason immediately dialed Patton.

"Captain Patton's."

"Mary, this is Jason. Is John still in?"

"Yes. Hold on, Jason."

A minute later, Patton picked up. "What's up?"

"I just got a call from Devin James."

"What now?"

"He said the story is front-page tomorrow morning."

"Dang it! That guy is a pain in my you-know-what!"

"I stuck with the no comment."

"Good. I have to go, but I'll talk to you in the morning."

"Have a good night, John."

The captain snorted. "Yeah, right!"

****

After an unknown number of hands of Gin, and a burned pizza she still ate most of, Tammy-Jo was back in front of the TV. He had turned on the set, and after she was

71

seated, plopped into his own chair. They had watched for nearly two hours and it appeared his eyes were getting heavy.

She would sneak a glance to her right, trying not to make a sound. If he fell asleep, she could run. She had already spotted a door at the far end of the kitchen; she just needed her chance.

She looked.

Did his eyes just close?

She checked again.

His eyes are shut!

She scooted the TV tray from in front of her to clear her path, then checked him again.

Still shut!

Slowly, she began to rise and was almost standing, when he snored. He'd woken himself up, and when he saw her standing, leapt from his chair. Tammy-Jo didn't have time to react. He was behind her, knife drawn and across her throat, in a flash.

"Thought you could sneak out, eh?"

Terrified, she struggled to keep him calm. "No...no. I just needed to use the bathroom!"

The blade eased slightly against her skin. "Go then!"

He released her and she bolted for the bathroom. When she came out, he was waiting at the end of the hall.

"Let's go."

Her pulse surged as he pointed toward the box room. He stepped out of the way as she approached and let her go to the makeshift coffin. She held her breath and lay down inside, the robe still on. The lid closed over her and the padlock snapped.

She was safe. For the night.

****

Jennifer Landers leaned against the bar, the fifth one she'd visited that night. In her hand was a copy of the sketch, done by the Police artist, based on her description. Every business along the River Walk had one in their window or at the counter. So far, there had been no calls to the hotline number.

Each of the last few nights, she had brought her copy of the sketch and hung around the bars looking for the surfer guy. It was the only thing she could think to do in an effort to find her friend. Two days from now she was supposed to be on an airplane home to Nebraska, back to her classes and the busyness of college, but she couldn't imagine leaving without her best friend.

Detective Warren had been keeping in touch with her, and she appreciated how

73

hard he was working to find Tammy-Jo, but frustration was building for both of them. Jennifer suspected the detective knew more than he was saying, but she didn't push; she didn't want to be shut out of the loop altogether.

"You want something to drink?"

Jennifer turned to see a sharp-looking bartender, in a white dress shirt and plaid bowtie, smiling at her. She checked his nametag.

"No thanks, Tommy." She slid the sketch across the bar. "Hey, have you seen this guy?"

Tommy glanced at it. "That's the same one in the window, right?"

"Yeah."

"No, I haven't seen him, but…"

Jennifer froze. "But?"

"Well, it doesn't look much like him to me, but the description of the surfer clothes reminds me of a guy who hangs out at the RainTree."

"Do you know his name?"

"No, but whenever I go by there, he's usually around."

Jennifer had been to the RainTree numerous times and not seen him. "Anybody you know at RainTree who might help me?"

"I don't know if she can help, but you

can ask for Jacy. She's been a waitress there for a long time."

"Jacy? Do you know her last name?"

"No, I'm sorry."

"Okay, Tommy. Thanks."

Jennifer raced outside and back toward the RainTree Restaurant. It took her less than five minutes to get there and she went straight to the maître d's desk. A tall girl, with raven hair and olive skin, was taking names for the tables. Jennifer had to wait in line to speak to her.

"How many in your party?"

Jennifer shook her head. "I don't need a table. Can you tell me if Jacy is working tonight?"

"No, she's on vacation."

Jennifer's heart sank. "Crap."

"Are you a friend of hers?"

"No, I just need to show her this picture." She held it up. "You don't happen to know who this is, do you?"

"No. I've seen the picture, but I've only worked here a couple weeks."

"Do you know when Jacy works next?"

The girl looked down at a book, flipped a page, then back up at Jennifer. "She's on vacation for another three days."

"Okay, thanks. I'm just going to sit at the bar for awhile."

75

LET'S PLAY

"That's fine."

Jennifer spent the rest of the night watching the door for the surfer guy. At one in the morning, she headed back to her hotel, without learning his name.

CHAPTER 6

Mary didn't greet John Patton with her usual smile. This morning was not off to a good start.

"Morning, Mary."

"Good morning, Captain. Chief wants you upstairs immediately."

"Crap."

He turned and walked back into the elevator, pushing the button for the fourth floor. He didn't bother asking why the chief wanted to see him; he'd already seen the front page. He pulled the newspaper from under his arm and looked at the headline again.

MELINDA GOMEZ MISSING NO MORE.

Body of the first River Walk girl is found.

77

LET'S PLAY

A picture of Gomez sat below the headline. She wore her high school graduation cap and gown along with a big smile, her arm around her mother. He folded the paper back up as the elevator doors opened.

Chief Murray's aide gave him a grim smile and went back to her work as John walked into the office. The chief was on the phone, standing near the window, but pointed at a chair.

"I understand, sir… I will… I'll call you as soon as I know anything."

The chief was less put-together this morning, his tie loose, and his shirt untucked; Patton suspected Murray had been here for a couple hours. Sitting quietly, he waited while the phone call ended, and Murray tucked in his shirt. The tie remained loose.

Murray moved behind his desk. "Do you want to guess who that was?"

"The mayor?"

"Do you want to guess what he was calling about?"

"The news story?"

"You're two for two, how about his last words before he hung up?"

"Have a good morning?"

The joke caught the chief by surprise and he laughed, despite his obvious stress level. "I wish. No, it was more like *I want someone's head!*"

"That was my next guess."

The chief dropped into his chair with a sigh. "He said he'd checked his end and the leak didn't come from city hall. Therefore, it must have come from our end and he wants to know who it was."

"I've spoken with everyone involved. Warren, Banks, Davis, Doc Josie. Each one insists they were tight-lipped."

"What about the new guy?"

"Darrel Chase?"

"Yeah, did you talk to him?"

"Yes, and he was very forthcoming. He knows he's the new guy and that puts him on the spot, but he assures me he didn't speak to anyone."

"Alright, tell everyone the lid is still on, despite what's in the paper, and jobs are on the line."

"I'll be sure they understand."

"Now, what about the case itself? Have we made any headway?"

"Eli Warren has the River Walk plastered with flyers of the surfer guy but nothing yet. Jason and Vanessa are rechecking everything in the Gomez file and cross checking with the other three missing."

"So, nothing."

79

LET'S PLAY

"Come on, Bill, you know how these things work. Cases that are going cold tend to have the thing you're looking for already in the file. It takes fresh eyes and luck to find it."

The chief sat quietly, regarding his captain. Finally, he smiled. "You would never have my job, would you?"

"Only if it came with a bullet to the head on day one."

Murray laughed. "I understand. Keep me up to speed."

Patton stood. "You're the first, Chief."

****

Jason and Vanessa were in the conference room by six that morning. There was still a lot of video to look at, files to go through, and no time to spare. They were on their third surveillance video when there was a knock and the captain entered, followed by Lieutenant Banks.

Jason shut off the video. "Good morning, Captain."

"Not so far. I gather you've seen the newspaper."

"Yes."

"Chief Murray has asked me to re-enforce the fact that this is still a low-

80

visibility investigation, and need-to-know is still in effect, despite the story in the paper."

Banks and both her detectives nodded.

"He also wanted to pass on that if there's another leak, or if they find who's responsible for today's front page, he will have them terminated."

Again, three silent nods.

Patton pointed at the whiteboard, where some notes were scribbled in Vanessa's handwriting. "What have you got?"

Vanessa stood and moved over to the board. She pointed with the marker in her hand as she talked.

"In watching the video, we've come up with three commonalities for each of the missing girls, prior to number four. We haven't looked at the video of Tammy-Jo Cousins yet. The first is a River Walk employee who had contact with at least two of the girls on the nights they went missing. He was interviewed, but we want to talk to him again. The second is the taxi stand. Each victim was in the vicinity of the taxi stand, although we only know for sure that one girl got in a cab."

Patton stopped her. "What about the cab logs?"

"We have copies, and they seem to provide an alibi for each cabbie on duty, but

81

only one driver worked all three nights.
We're still waiting for a log of the fourth
night. We want to speak to that cabbie again,
as well."

"What's the third link?"

"The RainTree Restaurant. We know
each girl was there at some time on the night
they went missing."

"Have employees been interviewed?"

Jason nodded. "There's page after
page of interviews, but we're still working
our way through those. So far, nothing
stands out."

Banks swiveled in her chair to look at
Jason. "What about the cemetery guy?"

"He's a loose end. We know he dug
the grave that Melinda Gomez was found in,
and he performs the same duties at five other
cemeteries. So far, that's his only connection
to the case."

"Did the phone records for the Cousins
girl come back?"

"Yes. The phone went dead the night
she disappeared. The last ping was in the
area of the River Walk."

There was another knock at the door.
Jason reached over and turned the knob.
"Hi, Eli. What's up?"

"I may have a lead on our surfer guy."

"Oh?"

"You remember the girl who reported

Tammy-Jo Cousins missing?"

"Sure."

"She called me this morning with the name Jacy Lennox; a waitress at the RainTree. She may know the guy in our sketch, so I spoke to the restaurant and they gave me her information. I'm on my way to talk to her now."

Vanessa stood. "You want some company?"

"I thought you guys might want to tag along."

Jason also got up. "Tag along? Heck, I'll drive!"

****

Jacy Lennox lived northwest of the city, on Briarcliff Road in the Castle Hills Subdivision, with her husband and two children. Castle Hills had wide streets, large old-growth trees, and brick ranch-style homes on large lots. It was one of Jason's favorite neighborhoods and he took Sandy to look at several homes in the area before they finally bought their place in Terrill Hills.

Jason found the address and parked on the street. Vanessa leaned on the hood of the car while Jason and Eli went up to the door. Eli pushed the bell and a resonant *ding-dong* echoed through the door. Within moments, they heard shuffling feet.

The door was opened by a woman in her early thirties with jet black hair pulled into a ponytail. "Can I help you?"

Jason showed his badge. "Jacy Lennox?"

"Yes."

"My name is Detective Strong and this is Detective Warren. We wanted to ask you a few questions, if that's okay."

"Is this about those missing girls?"

"Yes, ma'am."

"Do you want to come in?"

"Please."

She led the detectives down a tiled foyer to the rear of the house, where they entered a large family room. The TV was on to *The Price is Right*, but Jacy shut it off immediately.

"Can I get you some coffee?"

Jason shook his head as did Eli. "No, thank you."

They each took a seat on a large sectional, the detectives on one end of the L-shaped couch, and Jacy on the other.

Eli took out his notepad. "You're on vacation, is that right?"

"Yes, since last week."

"So you haven't seen this sketch?" Jason handed it to her.

84

"No…but he's not familiar."

Jason and Eli exchanged looks. "What about the written description?"

Jacy read it, and then looked up at the detectives. "Well, the picture doesn't look much like him, but the outfit sounds exactly like Denny."

"Denny?"

"Yeah, Dennis Purdom. He's been one of my regulars for years. His folks have money, so he doesn't work. He dresses like a surfer and hangs out, but seems pretty harmless. I think he even dyes his hair blonde for the image, but of course, there's nowhere to surf in San Antonio."

Jason handed her a missing flyer with all the women on it. "Did you ever see him in contact with any of these girls?"

She studied the pictures, then shook her head. "No, not that I can remember."

Something about the man's name seemed familiar to Jason.

"Dennis Purdom? Of the Purdom Construction family?"

"Yeah, that's them."

Jason stood and handed her his card. "Thank you very much. We won't trouble you any longer."

"No trouble."

Back outside, Jason and Eli found Vanessa sitting in the car with the A/C

85

running. Jason grinned at his partner as he climbed in. "Guess who our guy is?"

"I give up."

"Dennis Purdom, he goes by Denny."

"Purdom, like the construction Purdoms?"

"The same. They live in Scenic Oaks."

"Wow. Is that where we're going now?"

"It is."

"Awesome. I love the houses in that neighborhood."

Eli gave her a funny look and Jason laughed. "Never been, Eli?"

He shook his head.

Vanessa laughed. "Oh, you're gonna love this."

****

Scenic Oaks was north of San Antonio proper, just west of I-10, and mind-boggling to the average man or woman. Houses, better known as estates, began at seven figures and went way up from there. Jason and Vanessa had done an interview in a home that sold for six million dollars. It was mid-priced in this area, where tennis courts, pools, and hot tubs were mandatory to keep up with the neighbors.

On their way, Eli called in a record request on Dennis Purdom. As the result was given to him, he wrote it down. Hanging up, he filled in the other detectives.

"Two arrests for DUI, one for Public Intoxication, nothing as far as violent crime."

As they drove into the Scenic Oaks area, Vanessa watched Eli, laughing out loud when his mouth dropped open. One house after another on the tree-lined cul-de-sacs brought the exclamation of "Look at that one!"

When they finally reached the Purdom home, they had to stop at an automatic gate. Jason pushed the intercom.

"Yes?"

He looked at the camera hanging from the portico above them, and held up his badge. "Detective Jason Strong to speak with Dennis Purdom."

"Wait, please."

After several minutes, the speaker crackled to life at the same time as the automatic gate began to open. "Mr. Purdom will meet you at the main house."

Jason followed the long cobblestone drive as it wound its way up hill through the tall trees on either side. At the top, the hill crested and opened into a large parking area with a spraying fountain in the center. The house itself was modeled after an old English estate, complete with stained glass windows and steel framed doors.

Vanessa and Eli echoed each other. "Unbelievable."

Waiting for them on the marble steps was Dennis Purdom. His surfer outfit, which apparently wasn't just for cruising the bar scene, was a dead giveaway. The three detectives climbed out of the car and approached him, Eli leading the way. "Dennis Purdom?"

"That's me; Denny will do." He shook hands with the detective.

"My name is Detective Warren; this is Detective Strong and Detective Layne."

Denny shook hands with each but didn't offer to take them inside. "What brings you guys out here?"

"We're investigating the disappearance of four women from the River Walk area."

"I heard about that; I saw one was found dead."

"That's correct. Did you know Melinda Gomez?"

"No."

"I understand you like to go to the RainTree on a regular basis."

"Yeah, but there's no crime in that."

Jason sensed a defensive tone creeping into the man's voice. Eli kept it light.

"No, no, of course not. We were just wondering if you may have met Melinda at the RainTree."

"Like I said, she's not familiar. Is it possible? Sure, I guess."

Vanessa produced copies of the missing fliers and handed them to Denny. "What about these other women? Recognize any of them?"

He shuffled through them quickly and Jason picked up an almost imperceptible hesitation at the last flyer, the one of Tammy-Jo Cousins.

Denny shook his head. "Nope, none of them."

Jason took the fliers back, pulled out the last one, and held it up. "You sure she doesn't look familiar?"

Denny had re-gathered himself. "Nope."

"What's going on, Denny?"

Purdom and the detectives turned to look in the direction of the voice. Standing in the doorway was a tall woman with swept-up brown hair and bright blue eyes. She wore a yellow tennis skirt and a white tank top. Jason recognized her from the newspaper as Barbara Purdom.

"Nothing, Mom. These detectives were just asking some questions about those missing girls."

89

LET'S PLAY

The woman's face went from smiling to a blank stare in an instant. "I need you inside, Denny."

Denny shrugged and grinned at the detectives. "Momma knows best."

She waited until her son was in the house before directing her attention to the visitors. "Detectives, I'm afraid you'll have to leave. If you have any more questions, please make an appointment with our attorney."

She turned, walked inside, and the large front door closed behind them.

The detectives headed down the driveway as Vanessa said what they all were thinking. "What a pleasant lady."

Eli laughed. "Yeah, she went from zero to angry in record time."

Jason was more interested in the result of the questioning. "He denies remembering Tammy-Jo, even though it was just a couple days ago he was talking to her. If Jennifer Landers can ID him, we'll have ourselves a liar. Let's go by the station and get a mug shot for Jennifer to look at."

****

Vanessa offered to take the photo out to the hotel while Jason and Eli looked at some more video. She found Jennifer in her room packing. Vanessa reached onto the bed, picked up a shirt and meticulously folded it, before handing it to the girl.

"When do you leave?"

"Tomorrow morning."

"We never reached Tammy-Jo's parents. Did you ever get them?"

"Yes, about an hour ago. They were on safari in South Africa. They're trying to book a flight here and I gave them your number."

"I've got a photo I'd like you to look at. Do you mind?"

"No, of course not. Is it the surfer guy?"

Vanessa handed her the mug shot. "You tell me."

Jennifer's eyes widened. "That's him!"

"And you saw him dancing with Tammy-Jo the night she disappeared?"

"Yes."

"How long would you say they were together?"

"Oh, I don't know. Forty-five minutes or an hour, maybe. What's his name?"

"Dennis Purdom."

"Denny! I knew it was something like that. Does he know where Tammy-Jo is?"

"If he does, he's not saying."

"Well, can't you beat him up or

LET'S PLAY

something?"

Vanessa laughed. "I'm afraid not; that's only on TV. We don't even know if he's involved for sure, and besides, we only use water torture!"

It took a second for Jennifer to catch on. "You're teasing me, aren't you?"

"Yes, but we have questioned him and probably will again."

"Good."

Vanessa put her arm around the young girl. "Call me before you take off, okay?"

"I will."

She looked into the girls eyes. "And Jennifer..."

"Yeah?"

"I won't give up until I find Tammy-Jo."

Jennifer's eyes welled up with emotion she'd kept trapped too long. "Thank you."

Vanessa pulled her in and let her cry.

CHAPTER 7

When Vanessa returned to the station, she went directly to the third floor conference room. Jason and Eli sat in the dark watching the grainy black-and-white images move across the screen. Jason paused the video when she entered. "What did you find out?"

"She identified him immediately."

"And Jennifer previously told us she talked to Purdom before closing, when she left RainTree to look for Tammy-Jo, correct?"

"Yes."

Jason rewound the video, figures moving in fast backward motion until Jason stopped it again.

"Look what we found. We have Tammy-Jo coming out for a cigarette, followed by Denny Purdom, who joined her."

The tape moved forward and Vanessa

LET'S PLAY

watched it play out. After a few minutes, Tammy-Jo throws away her cigarette and returns to the bar. Denny leaves and heads toward the parking lot. The cameras lose him as he goes by the cab stand.

Jason stopped the tape on the last image of Denny. "Purdom is lying about not seeing Tammy-Jo and his time is unaccounted for from this point until Jennifer talked to him around closing.

Vanessa grabbed a chair and sat down. "What *about* Tammy-Jo? Do you have her leaving the bar?"

"No, at least not yet. She appears earlier, again having a smoke, where she's seen talking to a guy emptying the trash cans. He shows up on the Melinda Gomez tapes, but we haven't found him on the other two."

"Do we know his name?"

"Anthony Martinez. He's worked at the River Walk for almost a year."

"Is there another way to place him at work on the River Walk when the other two girls went missing?"

Eli stood. "I can handle that. I'll go to the offices of the River Walk and request his time cards."

"Good."

When Eli left, Jason restarted the video. Vanessa was bothered by the lack of

94

further video on Tammy-Jo.

"How would our girl get out of the bar and not be seen?"

"It's possible she went along the back walkway, which doesn't have video. It's used mainly by employees and delivery people, and there's no city closed circuit."

"Well, if she did leave that way, she either had a lift from someone or took a cab, right?"

"Probably."

"Have we checked with all the drivers from that night?"

"Eli said he had not received the driver logs yet."

"Then perhaps we should go see what the delay is."

Jason shut off the video player, and stood. "Perhaps we should. I've got the driver logs from the nights the other three girls went missing. If we can match a fourth, it might narrow things some more."

****

The main garage and headquarters for San Antonio Blue Cab was located near downtown on Lone Star Boulevard. They parked on the street and entered through the open garage door. Cabs were parked in long

LET'S PLAY

rows with their lights dark, except for a couple cars getting ready to start their shifts.

A bald man nearly as wide as he was tall shouted at them as they approached. "No civilians inside the garage!"

Jason took out his badge, flashing it for the man, then tucked it away. "Official police business."

The man was unimpressed. "What now?"

Jason glanced at the nameplate partially covered by a sandwich wrapper on the desk.

"Well Frank, I need some information, and I'm guessing you're just the one to help."

"You're guessing wrong; I'm just the dispatcher. If you want information, go through that door, and ask for Lucy."

Both detectives turned their heads in the direction he pointed. A glass door led out of the garage into an office. "Okay, Frank. Thanks."

Frank didn't respond, putting his head down and continuing his paperwork.

Jason held the door open for Vanessa and they entered into a space too small to contain all the smoke from Lucy's cigarette. Vanessa coughed, waving her hand in front of her. Lucy stubbed out her lit butt.

"Sorry, I'm in here alone most of the

96

day."

Jason propped the door open and held it while Vanessa talked to auburn-haired woman.

Vanessa showed her badge. "My name is Detective Layne with SAPD. Frank said you're who I need to talk to for information."

Lucy grunted. "Yeah, Frank helps nobody. What do you need?"

"We're after the logs of your drivers from three nights ago. The department sent over a request, but we haven't received them."

"I don't remember any paperwork; Frank probably threw it away. What's this about?"

"We're just doing some background on a murder case."

"The Gomez thing?"

"Yes."

Lucy had opened a file cabinet and pulled a folder. "That was awful, them finding her dead and all."

Vanessa nodded as she accepted the thick folder. "Do you have certain cabs assigned to the River Walk?"

"Yeah. They work our stand over there."

"Can you give me a copy of just those logs?"

97

LET'S PLAY

"Sure." She took the folder back and went over to a copy machine. "Just a minute."

Vanessa moved over by the open door for a breath of air. When the copies were done, she returned to get them from Lucy. "Thank you for your help."

"No problem. Sorry again about the smoke."

Outside in the car, Jason looked over his records as Vanessa read the names from three nights ago. "Jesse Thomas?"

Jason shook his head.

"Michael Ware?"

Another shake of the head.

"Julie Masters?"

Head shake. It went on like this for several minutes; name after name not cross-matching the other three cases. Some had one case in common but not all four. Vanessa kept reading.

"Ricardo Bonitez?"

There was a hesitation. "Yes. He's on duty all three of these nights, which makes him the only one so far."

Vanessa finished the list, not finding another name that matched. Bonitez would need further investigation. Jason's phone started to ring.

"This is Strong."

Vanessa listened but couldn't make out

who it was. Jason nodded a couple times, his glance coming over to Vanessa, then down to his list. "Things are looking up, Eli. We've got a name to check out ourselves. See you at the station in the morning."

Jason closed his phone. "Eli said the worker at River Walk shows up on the time card all four nights."

"Really? You're right; things are looking up."

****

Fear surged through Tammy-Jo with the unlocking of the box. It had become her safe place, and even with the claustrophobia, she preferred it to being with him. By her best estimate, she was near the end of her third day in captivity.

He hadn't left her hungry or thirsty, but the physical abuse was worse than either of those. The lid flipped open and he stood there, smiling. "Let's play."

She didn't move. "Play what?"

"Oh, I don't know. How about Yahtzee?"

Tammy-Jo knew the game; she and Jennifer had played it on the airplane. He extended his hand to her. "Out you get."

She pulled herself up, refusing his

99

LET'S PLAY

help.

Just like the nights before, food was waiting at the table, along with water. After they'd eaten, he brought the game over from the shelf and set it down. "You know how to play?"

She nodded.

"Good. I'll keep score and you can go first."

She picked up the cup with five dice in it and rolled them out onto the table. Mechanically, she slid two off to the side and gathered up the three remaining. She rolled them and repeated the procedure. After the third roll, she made a choice. "Twenty-three in chance."

He marked it down, gathered up the dice, and dropped them into the cup. He shook the cup for a long time, which vibrated against her frayed nerves, before finally rolling them. He then mimicked her steps in dice choice.

It went on like that for three hours. At the end of the fifth game, Tammy-Jo was exhausted. "I don't want to play anymore."

Without a word, he gathered up three of the dice and the score sheet, putting them into the box. The cup remained on the table and he dropped the last two dice into it.

"Now's the time for the real game."

Fear shot through her. "What do you

mean?"

His eyes bored into her. "Have you ever played Craps?"

"No…I don't think so."

"Well, you're going to play now. One round and if you win, it's your choice. If I win, it's mine."

"Choice of what?"

He held up a finger. "In a minute; first the rules."

He tumbled the dice out onto the table. "A two and a four. That's six."

"Yeah, so?"

"So, now you'll roll. You have to get a total of six, any way you can, before you roll a seven."

Her heart was pounding. "What if I get a seven?"

"Then you crap out and I win."

"And if I get the six first?"

"You win."

"What's the prize?"

"You are."

Tears welled up in her eyes. "What do you mean?"

"Crap out and your body is mine tonight. Get a six, you can choose to go back to the box."

"What if I don't want to roll?"

"Then you lose automatically." His hand went to the handle of his knife, resting

101

there for emphasis. "What is your decision?"

She didn't have a choice; she had to roll.

Slowly, she put the dice back in the cup, shook it once, and turned it over. The dice cascaded out onto the table. As if in slow motion, she watched a five come up, and then a two roll over into a three. She felt herself breathe.

He clapped his hands together, causing her to jump. "Eight, roll again!"

She repeated the steps, watching this time as a five was followed by a four.

"Nine, roll again!"

This time she moved faster, just wanting the twisted game to end. The dice hit the table, scurrying away from her. A five appeared first and was followed by a one, which hesitated for a second, before rolling over into a two.

"Craps! I win!"

Tammy-Jo shuddered and her tears overflowed. The hope of escaping her captor's hands cruelly dashed by a roll of the dice.

CHAPTER 8

Eli decided not to go to the station the next morning, but instead he drove directly to the address he had for Anthony Martin. The apartment was on the ground floor of a three-story complex in desperate need of paint and landscaping. Eli expected the inside of the building to look no better and he was right. Taking the dimly lit hallway, he checked numbers until about halfway along he found the apartment.

Eli knocked and waited. It took a long time before any noise indicated someone was home. A sleepy Martin opened the door. "Yeah?"

"Anthony Martin?"

"Yeah. Who are you?"

Eli held up his badge. "Detective Warren, SAPD. Can I speak to you for a minute?"

Martin suddenly appeared more awake. "Uh, I guess."

LET'S PLAY

"Mind if I come in?"

Martin looked back over his shoulder, and then stepped into the hall. "Actually, my girlfriend is asleep. I'd rather talk out here so we don't wake her."

"Okay." Eli took out his notepad. "Does your girlfriend live with you?"

"Yeah."

"What's her name?"

Martin appeared unnerved. "Why does that matter?"

"Just background."

"Look, Detective...Warren is it?"

"Yes."

"Well, why don't you get to the point? I work nights and would like to go back to bed."

Eli produced some flyers. "Do you recognize any of these girls?"

Martin took a quick look at the posters. "This again? I answered all these questions before."

The detective held out the Tammy-Jo Cousins flyer. "This girl went missing four days ago. Do you remember her?"

Martin looked again. "No."

"I have you on video talking to her on the night she disappeared."

"Detective, I talk to a lot of women at work. They're all over the River Walk at night while I'm cleaning."

"So you don't remember talking to her?"

"No. Can I go back to bed now?"

Eli folded up the flyers and put them away. "Thank you for your time, Mr. Martin. Here's my card, and I would appreciate a call if you think of anything that might be helpful."

Without another word, Martin took the card, went back into the apartment, and shut the door.

****

When Eli let them know he was going to the Martin apartment, Jason and Vanessa headed out to speak with Ricardo Bonitez. As they drove, Vanessa compared the log sheets.

"This is interesting."

"What's that?"

"Bonitez took lunch at nearly the exact same time on all four dates, and his lunch was more than two hours."

"Yeah, so?"

"Wouldn't you think cabbies eat on the run, or at the very least, when there was no fares?"

Jason thought about it for a minute. "I guess. Maybe you should call Lucy and ask

105

her what's normal."

"Good idea. I knew there was a reason I let you hang around."

The line rang twice before being picked up. "Blue Cab."

Vanessa was pretty sure she could smell smoke through the phone. "Lucy?"

"Yes, this is Lucy."

"This is Detective Layne; we spoke to you yesterday."

"Of course, what can I do for you?"

"I have a general question. Is it normal for a driver to take a lunch?"

"Normal? I guess. Most will eat in between fares, usually sitting in the cab."

"So, would two hours be considered a long lunch?"

"Very. The drivers only make money when they're taking fares."

"Okay. Thanks for the time."

"You bet."

Vanessa hung up and looked at Jason. "She used the word 'very' to describe how unusual a two-hour lunch was."

Jason turned the car into a small subdivision and stopped in front a plain ranch home. "Here it is. I'd guess we're less than twenty minutes from the River Walk cab stand."

Vanessa studied the house. White painted stucco, grey roof shingles, and almost no landscaping. The garage door was closed and no vehicle was in the driveway. "That would leave him nearly an hour and a half to stash a girl on one of those lunch breaks."

While they sat there, the garage door started up, and a white minivan backed out. Jason jumped from the car. "It's him."

He did a slow trot to a point where he could speak through the driver's side window as Vanessa came up on the passenger side. Jason showed his badge while Vanessa moved slowly around the vehicle, looking in the windows. When she had gone all the way around, she joined Jason on the driver's side. He was having a hard time hearing Bonitez over the noisy van.

"Mr. Bonitez, would you mind shutting off the van?"

The man hesitated but then complied.

"Thank you. My partner and I would like to speak to you about some missing girls."

"From the River Walk?"

"Yes."

Bonitez rolled his eyes. "I've been through this over and over."

"Actually, I specifically want to ask you about four nights ago. Did you have a young girl as one of your fares?"

LET'S PLAY

Bonitez hesitated. "Yeah."

Vanessa and Jason exchanged looks. Jason produced the flyer of Tammy-Jo. "Was this her?"

A quick glance. "No."

"What time did you have this fare?"

"Around closing time. I took her to the Days Inn on East Houston."

Vanessa nudged Jason. "Probably Jennifer Landers."

"Mr. Bonitez, do you usually take a lunch during your shift?"

The cabbie looked confused, and Vanessa sensed he was trying to figure out what the best answer was. He opted for middle of the road.

"Sometimes."

"About an hour or so?"

"Sometimes, sometimes not that long."

"Do you ever take a two-hour lunch?"

"Uh…No. That would get me an earful from Frank."

Jason held up the log sheets he had in his hand. "Well, I found at least four times when you took a lunch of roughly two hours."

Bonitez did his best to keep his composure. "I don't know when I would've done that. It must be a mistake."

"How so?"

"I probably forgot to write down a

108

fare."

"But that could get you fired, couldn't it?"

"Look, I sometimes skip writing fares to make some extra cash. I'm not alone, lots of drivers do it. Please don't tell Frank."

Jason gave the log sheets to Vanessa and got out a card. "Here's my number. Call me if you remember anything else."

Bonitez took it. "Of course."

They left him sitting in the driveway and walked back to their car. Vanessa was suspicious. "He's hiding something."

"Yeah, but it might be just what he says. He's skimming from the cab company."

Vanessa wasn't convinced. "Maybe, maybe not."

****

Sarah Banks closed her office door and picked up the phone. A minute later, she heard his voice.

"Hello?"

"Hi, Gavin, it's me."

"Hey, I was just thinking about you."

She laughed. "You always say that when I call."

"Maybe because I'm always thinking

about you."

"That's very sweet. A lie, but sweet."

"Just trying to rack up the brownie points."

She laughed again. In fact, she noticed that since Gavin Newman came around, she laughed a lot. However, her reason for calling wasn't a laughing matter.

"Gavin, can I ask you something?"

"Of course, anything."

"It's a little sensitive and I don't want you to take it the wrong way."

"Okay…sounds serious."

"It is."

"Well, like I said, anything."

Sarah took a deep breath. "You would never share anything I told you in confidence with someone else, would you?"

Gavin didn't respond immediately, and when he did, there was an undercurrent to his voice. Sarah sensed she may have hurt him. "Are you asking if you can trust me?"

"No…yes. Gavin, I don't mean to suggest…"

"You're more than suggesting it."

Sarah began to panic, afraid she may have crossed some invisible line that would take Gavin from her. "Let me explain, please."

His silence signaled her to go ahead.

"A situation has come up here at work,

110

and it could cost someone their career. I want to make sure we're on the same page about things we discuss."

When he spoke again, he seemed calmer, his voice softer.

"Sarah, I would never do anything to hurt you, especially when it comes to your career. I promise I haven't said a word to anyone."

She allowed herself a smile. "I know. I'm sorry if I hurt you, I just had to be sure."

"I understand. Talk to you later?"

"I'll call you when I'm headed home."

She hung up, feeling better for asking, but still worried. There still might have been a forgotten slip that could cost her everything.

****

Jason took the bag of food from the drive-thru attendant and handed it to Vanessa. After getting their drinks, he rolled his window up, and pulled away.

They ate as he drove toward the station, not talking. Finally, with his burger gone, Jason asked the same question he'd asked at least once a week for the past few months.

"You and Rob doing okay?"

111

LET'S PLAY

She smirked as several fries disappeared into her mouth. "Yeah…we're trying again."

"I didn't know you ever stopped trying."

She laughed. "You know what I mean."

He did. After losing the baby, Vanessa had needed time to heal before trying to get pregnant again.

"I'm glad to hear it."

"What about you and Sandy?"

"What about us?"

"Are you ready for another little one?"

"She is and I guess I am. There's something very special about watching Nina with Penny. That big dog loves her, and is incredibly gentle when they play, but it makes me think Nina might like a brother."

"A brother?"

Jason laughed. "Yeah, I told Sandy if she got pregnant again, it had to be a boy."

"Ha! I bet she loved that."

"Her reaction was about the same as yours."

"So you're trying then?"

"Actually, did I ever tell you Nina was a surprise?"

"No."

"Yup, we were still being careful at the time. I figure it'll happen again and when it does, good."

He turned into the station parking lot just as Vanessa finished her fries. She gathered up the wrappers and they walked toward the building. "What now?"

"I think we catch up with Eli, then brief Banks."

She tossed the bag in a trash can. "Sounds good."

LET'S PLAY

CHAPTER 9

When they got off the elevator, Eli was sitting at Jason's desk. He stood, relinquishing the chair to its rightful owner. "Hey, you two. Did you find the cabbie?"

Jason nodded. "He says he never saw the girls. Did you find Martin?"

"Yeah, he doesn't remember the girls, but admits he may have talked to them. I believe he fancies himself a ladies' man."

Vanessa laughed. "You couldn't tell it from his photo."

"So what next?"

"I think it's time to run things past Banks. Let's see if she has an idea."

All three detectives got up, grabbed their notes, and went over to the office. Jason knocked and leaned through the door. "Lieutenant?"

She looked like she'd just gotten off the phone and seemed surprised to see him. "Jason, I didn't know you guys were back."

"We are. Got a few minutes?"

"Of course."

Jason went in and was followed by the other two. When Vanessa and Eli had grabbed a chair, Jason picked up a marker. Standing by the whiteboard at the end of the room, he started to write, explaining as he went.

"First victim, Melinda Gomez, went missing on December 15; she was buried on December 22. We know that based on the day the man above her was buried."

He dropped down a line.

"Victim two, Rosalind Garner, disappeared on January 24, her whereabouts unknown. Victim three, Joann Heddon, disappeared on February 27, her whereabouts also unknown."

He checked the piece of paper in his hand, then continued. "Tammy-Jo Cousins went missing on April 1, still missing."

He moved over to an open space and restarted at the top. "We have four people of interest. First, Anthony Martin. He's a worker on the River Walk and has had contact with at least two of the victims. We've confirmed he was working on the other two nights."

Banks interrupted. "Does he have an alibi?"

"Just that he talks to lots of girls."

115

LET'S PLAY

"That's not an alibi, what about his whereabouts at the time the girls disappeared?"

"He was on the clock, that's his alibi." Jason turned back to the board. "Second is Ricardo Bonitez. He's cab driver who worked all four nights but claims he never picked up any of the missing girls. His alibi is the cab logs, but there's a gap around the time each girl disappeared."

Banks stopped him again. "How does he explain that?"

"He says he was taking fares but not writing them down, skimming money from the cab company."

"That's mighty thin."

"Yes, but we can't place the girls *in* his cab. Thirdly, we have Dennis Purdom. He's had contact with at least two of the girls, Tammy-Jo and Melinda Gomez."

"What's his alibi?"

"We didn't really get one before his mother shut down the conversation."

"His mother?"

"Yes, perhaps you've heard of her. Barbara Purdom."

"Of Purdom Construction?"

Jason nodded.

"And she cut you off?"

"Like a slice of ham; she told us to call her lawyer."

"Interesting. Anyone else?"

Jason nodded. "Nathan Wolsey. He's the manager at the cemetery where Melinda Gomez was found. He dug the grave she was found in on the night before the funeral."

The lieutenant's eyebrows went up. "That's convenient, if you want to bury a body."

"Yes, but we only have the one body, which means we can only tie him to one victim, and possibly only by coincidence."

Jason sat down and all four stared at the board. Jason hoped somebody would see something he didn't. Eli hadn't said a word since they came in, and Jason recognized his blank stare; it matched the one he was wearing.

Vanessa also had been quiet, but the look on her face gave Jason hope. He could see the wheels turning. "What is it, Vanessa? Do you see something?"

"Well...we know from experience that most serial killers have a pattern, one they rarely deviate from, but here we don't have a clear indication of what his pattern is. Where the victims are missing from is a constant, but that's it."

"Okay, so?"

Vanessa stood and went to the board, pointing at the name Melinda Gomez. "Miss

117

LET'S PLAY

Gomez is the only one we have an end result, so what if we form the pattern based on her alone?"

"Okay…makes sense, but how?"

"Melinda went missing on December 15 and she was buried on December 21, because the funeral was on the twenty-second, right?"

Jason was trying to catch up to where his partner was going. "Right."

"So that gives us a window of six days before he killed her, or at least buried her. If we use that number from the day each of the other three went missing, we can assume Rosalind would have been buried on January 30, Joann on March 4, and finally, Tammy-Jo would be on April 6."

The room went silent as each detective realized what Vanessa's theory meant. The date was April 4, meaning they were looking for two more bodies, and might only have two days left to find Tammy-Jo.

Banks moved first. Pulling her laptop toward her, she punched in some words, then swung it toward the detectives. As they watched, a map of the San Antonio area came on the screen, followed by a series of little red dots that popped up like measles on the city.

Jason looked at the search window on the computer. "The dots are cemeteries?"

118

"Yes. The search shows roughly forty-five cemeteries."

She swung the computer back to her and made the map smaller, then turned it back so they all could see.

"If you assume that a cemetery in the middle of the city would attract too much attention to be digging around in after dark, then that leaves only nine cemeteries similar to San Isidro where victim one was found."

"But we can't search nine cemeteries, and if we could, how? You can't dig up all those graves."

Vanessa pointed at the board. "We have two dates, January 31 and March 5, when the funerals would have taken place. If the pattern holds, we need to search the graves of funerals held in the nine cemeteries on those two days!"

Jason was unconvinced. "Wow! That's a stretch."

Banks liked it. "It's all we've got. Do some research and let me know if you ID a grave you want to search."

"You'll dig it up?"

"Not if I can help it. You do your research and I'll work on a solution. I have an idea."

The detectives looked at each other, shrugged, and went to work. When they left the office, Banks was already on the phone.

119

LET'S PLAY

The best source for funerals was the
San Antonio News. Vanessa was able to pull
up past issues, including obituaries, on the
newspaper's website. Jason had placed a call
to Terry Orman at Blessed Grace funeral
home and learned that the number of deaths
on an average day in San Antonio is roughly
thirty. Not all had a funeral within a few
days, but it gave them an idea what the
scope of their search would be.

The first date Vanessa punched in was
January 31, and she found nineteen funerals
scheduled for the day. Jason had hung a map
of the San Antonio area up on the
conference room wall, and Eli had his laptop
open. Vanessa read off the cemetery name
for each funeral.

"Mission Park South."

Eli punched it into his computer.
"1700 Military Drive."

Jason was holding some pins, but
didn't move.

"San Fernando Cemetery One."

"1100 South Colorado."

Still another cemetery inside the
Highway 1604 Loop, no pin required. They
decided on using the 1604 Loop as their

120

boundary because outside that was where the countryside became much more rural.

"Holy Cross Cemetery."

"2628 Mission Road."

This address was marked, Jason using a red pin to signify the January 31 date. It went on like this until all nineteen were checked, and then Jason switched to yellow pins as Vanessa started with the listings from March 5. Just six pins were on the map when they were done; four red and two yellow.

Jason wrote the addresses down along with the contact numbers given to him by Eli. He looked at the list, then his partners. "I guess I'll go tell Banks what we've got."

He left the conference room and turned the corner, knocking on the lieutenant's door.

"Come!"

Jason opened the door and leaned in. "We've got six possible, Lieutenant."

"Let me see."

He handed her the note and waited while she studied the list.

"Okay, let's start with victim three. It's just two graves so I'm going to request permission to search those first. I'll let you know when I get the thumbs up."

Jason nodded and headed back out the door.

121

LET'S PLAY

****

John Patton sat at his desk signing requisition forms. Paperwork had been bad when he was in charge of Homicide, but as captain over multiple departments, he'd nearly lost his mind signing stuff the first few weeks on the job. Now, it was just part of the everyday routine.

His phone buzzed. "Patton."

It was Mary. "Lieutenant Banks is on two."

"Thanks." He pushed line two. "Hey, Sarah."

"Hi, John. I need to speak to you, mind if I come up?"

"That's fine. Maybe you could sign some of these forms for me while you're here."

"Your signature stuff is above my pay grade."

The captain laughed. "I wish it was above mine."

"I'll be right up."

Five minutes later, Patton heard a knock. "Come in."

Sarah Banks entered with a sheet of paper in her hand. She walked over and sat down in front of the captain's desk, sliding

122

the paper toward Patton.

"We're working a theory on the River Walk Missing. That list is of the cemeteries where we think we might find Rosalind Garner or Joann Heddon. I need permission to search the last two locations with GPR."

Patton was intrigued. "How did you come up with this list?"

"Long story short, we applied the pattern of Melinda Gomez to the other girls."

"Pattern?"

"Gomez was buried, six days after going missing, in a grave that was covered the next day."

Patton's bushy eyebrows went up. "Interesting. It's a bit of a stretch, but not a bad idea."

"Layne was the one who spotted it."

"She would. I'll sign off on it as long as you can secure the search tool."

"I already have a lead on one."

Patton laughed. "I thought you might. When do you plan on doing it?"

"First thing tomorrow."

"Good."

Banks got up, retrieved the note from Patton, and headed for the door. "Sarah?"

She turned. "Yeah?"

"Anything new on who was responsible for the press leak?"

123

LET'S PLAY

"No, John. Nothing."

"The chief is not letting it go, mostly because the mayor is not letting it go, which means I can't let it go."

"If I hear anything, you'll be my first call."

"Good. Let me know how the search goes."

****

Sarah took the stairs down to the third floor, then went straight to the conference room. She found the three detectives reviewing video again. She handed the list back to Jason as Vanessa turned on the lights.

"Patton has signed off on the searches; start out at Davenport Cemetery first thing tomorrow."

Vanessa looked at Jason, then Banks. "What are we doing, digging it up?"

"No. I'm arranging for a GPR unit to meet you there in the morning."

"GPR?"

"Ground-penetrating radar." Jason and Vanessa stared at Eli, who had piped up with the explanation.

"You've heard of it?"

"Sure. I've used them in missing

124

persons cases several times."

"How does it work?"

"You shoot radar in to the ground and an image of what's below comes back."

Vanessa wrinkled her nose. "That's creepy."

Banks turned to go. "Creepy or not, we use it tomorrow, nine sharp."

****

Tammy-Jo couldn't see a clock, but by now she could almost sense when he would be coming to get her. Her mind was telling her it would be soon, and sure enough, footsteps echoed on the hall floor outside the room. The steps were followed by the click of the doorknob, then the snap of the padlock being opened, and finally, the blinding light as the lid was lifted.

"Play time."

"I don't want to play."

His hand moved slightly from his hip to the knife handle. "Oh, sure you do."

Tammy-Jo forced herself not to panic. "No, not today."

The words had no sooner left her lips than the knife was resting across her throat, his face right next to hers, his breath filling her senses. "Are you sure?"

125

LET'S PLAY

She didn't answer, afraid her voice would fail her anyway, and slowly sat up while pushing the knife back with her fingers. He let her force it away but she cut her fingertip, almost like a paper cut, and it told her how sharp he kept his weapon.

He smiled as she climbed out of the box. "See, I knew you wanted to play. Go to the bathroom and then we can start."

Tammy-Jo caught sight of herself in the mirror. It was easy to see she was losing a little more of herself every day. Her face was thinner, her hair more matted, and the light in her eyes was ebbing slowly away. She was torn between wanting to survive and wishing it would all be over.

She staggered down the hall, relieved herself without bothering to shut the door, and returned. He waited for her to walk past him, and then followed her to the card table.

A sandwich sat on a plate, a glass of water next to it. In the middle of the table, a Monopoly board was set up. Money had been separated into two piles, the dice lay in the middle of the board, and the little silver car was sitting on 'GO'.

"You can choose your piece, but I want the car. What do you want?"

She didn't care, and was more interested in the food, but pointed at the shoe while eating. "That's…fine."

He placed it on 'GO,' handed her one die, and they rolled. He got a six and she a four.

"I'm first."

The game began, and like most games of Monopoly, it went on for a while. Despite her barely paying attention, it was three hours later when he declared himself the winner. Tammy-Jo slumped back into her chair, sensing what was next, but hoping she was wrong.

He slowly folded up the board, put away the money, but left out the dice. He rolled them onto the table. "Eight. Your turn."

She didn't bother to object, there was no point. She prayed she'd win this time and be left alone this night. "I need an eight before a seven, right?"

"Right."

She gathered up the dice and flung them on the table, one of them rolling onto the floor. The one on the table was a five, and when she looked at the floor, she saw a three. Her heart leapt into throat. "Eight! I win!"

He leaned over and picked up the die on the floor, laid it next to the other one on the table, and pointed at them. "Roll again."

"Why? I won."

"The dice have to stay on the table."

127

LET'S PLAY

"But…"

His look cut her off.

She reached for the dice, determined this time, even convinced she was going to win. She rolled them and watched a pair of threes come up.

"Six." His tone was flat.

She didn't wait, grabbing them quickly, she threw them again. A four and a…five.

"Nine."

Her adrenaline had surged. "I can add!"

He stared at her, but let the outburst go. "Again."

She grabbed the dice, tossed them so both rolled right up to the edge of the table, right under his nose. A six was followed by a…she watched it settle…two!

She beat him to the punch. "Eight!"

Her eyes met his with defiance, almost daring him to find another excuse, but she was surprised. A smile crept across his face, and he reached out to gather the dice. "Into the box; unless you would rather not."

She almost spat in his face. "The box will be fine."

When the lid was shut and the lock in place, Tammy-Jo broke into a grin. For just a fleeting minute, it was good to defeat him, to beat him at one of his own games. The

128

darkness quickly stole the joy from her victory, leaving her with the sense her time was running out.

LET'S PLAY

CHAPTER 10

The next morning, Jason and Vanessa were waiting at Davenport Cemetery for the GPR tech to show up, and at exactly nine o'clock, a blue van pulled in through the front gate. The lettering on the side declared Texas Archeology Services had arrived.

The driver, a man around thirty with black hair and a matching black beard, got out sporting white coveralls. He walked to the rear of the van and opened the doors. The detectives went over and peered in.

"Is that it?"

The man turned and looked at them. "Are you Strong and Layne?"

"Yes."

"Hi, I'm Buddy Tanner. Yeah, that's it."

"It looks like an oversized orange lawnmower."

Buddy laughed. "It rolls like one too, but that's about the only similarity. Where do you want me to search?"

Jason pointed in the direction of the grave they'd found earlier. "Over there."

"Okay. Give a few minutes to set up and we'll start."

"Good enough."

Jason followed Vanessa back over by the grave they were to search. The stone bore the name Gloria Gaston, the woman who had been buried here on March 5. It was a flat stone, about a foot square, and had taken them nearly a half hour to find.

Jason stood looking down at the ground and his mind went to an old fairytale. "Hey Vanessa, you think it's like the princess and the pea?"

"Is what like that?"

"You know, Miss Gaston can tell something is under her."

Vanessa shook her head. "You're nuts, Strong."

"Why is it that both women in my life keep telling me I'm nuts?"

"Because you are."

"Oh."

Buddy came walking over to where they stood, pushing the four-wheeled contraption ahead of him. It looked exactly like a lawn mower, except where the engine should be there was just a small hump, and on the mower-like handle was a miniature

131

LET'S PLAY

TV screen.

"Is this the grave?"

Vanessa nodded. "Yes. So how does this work, anyway?"

"Well, first I'll mark off a series of squares on the grass, then move from one to the next and pulse the ground."

"And the screen will show a picture of a skeleton?"

Buddy smiled. "No, I'm afraid not. That's a made-for-TV depiction of how these work. What it does is show disturbances in the soil pattern. So the grave will show up like an upside-down 'U,' which is a reflection of the anomaly below the surface."

"How deep can it see?"

"It varies greatly by the kind of soil, and since most of this area is limestone, about fifty feet is usually the max depth."

Jason patted the man on the shoulder. "That's enough for us. You get started and let us know what you find."

"Okay."

Jason's phone rang. "Strong."

"Good morning, Jason. Is the GPR guy there?"

Jason mouthed the name Banks to Vanessa. "Yeah, Lieutenant. He's just getting started."

"Okay, well don't bug him; I'm paying

132

him by the hour."

Jason burst out laughing and turned to Vanessa. "Banks said not to bug the guy because *she's* paying him by the hour! That's awful nice of you, Lieutenant."

"Okay, okay, I'm not, but the department is."

"Understood. We'll let you know if he comes up with anything."

He hung up and the detectives stood watching Buddy work with the sensor. He went up one side of the grave, stopping every foot or so, then worked his way down from the headstone. At the base of the grave, he turned and worked his way back up, before coming down the far side.

When he was done, he pushed a few buttons, and retraced the base of the grave, going back and forth across where Gloria's feet would be. Finally, he waved the detectives over to where he stood.

"What were you hoping to find?"

Jason began to hope they may have got lucky. "A second body buried beneath the first."

Buddy's surprise was evident on his face. "I see. Well, I don't see any indication of a second body. The single coffin comes back pretty clear, but that's all."

"Okay. We've got five more to check so we better get going."

133

LET'S PLAY

"Where's the next one?"

Vanessa pulled out her notepad.

"Black Hill Cemetery, southwest of town."

"Okay, I'll follow you guys."

****

Twenty-five minutes later, they pulled into Black Hill Cemetery. Much smaller than Davenport, it only took a few minutes to find the headstone. While Buddy was setting up his grid and preparing to do the search, another vehicle pulled up. Jason was surprised by who stepped out.

"Nathan, right?"

"Yes. You're Detective Strong, aren't you?"

"What are you doing here?"

"This is one of the cemeteries I manage for the board. My boss called and told me to be here when you guys do your search."

"Well, you're just in time; the search is just about to start."

"My boss said you wouldn't be digging up the grave. How are you going to search then?"

"We've got a radar setup that will do the job."

"Oh, wow. Okay."

Jason was watching Nathan very carefully but didn't sense any nervousness, just curiosity.

After just a few minutes of searching, Buddy waved the detectives over. When they were standing next to him, he pointed at the screen while he moved the photo forward and back.

"You see that upside-down U shape there?"

They both nodded.

"Now watch just below it."

Jason's pulse sped up as a second upside-down U flashed onto the screen. "Is that another body?"

Buddy shook his head. "I can't say that. What it shows is there is a second disturbance of the soil, below the initial grave. Could it be a body? Yes. Is it a body? I don't know."

"Okay, Buddy. Pack up and get ready to go to the next cemetery."

"But I'm not done here."

"Yes you are." He pulled his phone and dialed Banks.

"This is Banks."

"This is Jason. We've got a hit. Black Hill Cemetery and I need a search warrant."

"Okay, I'll send it out with Detective Warren."

"Good. Can I send Eli with the GPR

135

tech and keep Vanessa here with me while we dig?"

"Yes. Is there someone at the cemetery who can do the digging?"

Jason looked over at Nathan Wolsey who was watching from his truck. "Yes and no."

"I'm sorry?"

"Nathan Wolsey, the cemetery manager is here, but he's on the suspect list. I don't think we should have him digging around what could be his own crime scene."

"Definitely not. I'll send a highway department backhoe."

"We'll be waiting."

****

It was after lunch before Eli had shown up with the warrant, then left with the GPR tech for the next grave at Emmanuel Lutheran Cemetery. Nathan Wolsey had called his boss when he received the search warrant, and she'd asked for him to bring it to her. By the time he returned, the backhoe was in place and beginning to dig.

Jason was overseeing the backhoe operator as he scraped at the grave, removing the dirt, and getting prepared to lift the coffin. The going was slow because

136

the operator was not accustomed to digging up graves, and was clearly nervous.

Vanessa at off to the side watching Nathan as the digging proceeded. She wanted to catch the reaction of the cemetery manager as the grave was uncovered. If they did find Joann Heddon's body below the coffin, Nathan's reaction could lead them to focus on him or rule him out.

She decided to walk over and sit right next to him. "No problem with the search warrant?"

He shook his head, not looking away from the digging. "Mrs. Fulton said it looked legit and told me to come back here. I'm supposed to report to her after you're done."

"Did the hole get filled in at San Isidro?"

"Yeah, I did it yesterday. Do you think there's another body under this grave?"

"We don't know. The test showed something irregular and so we have to look."

"I hope there isn't. It would freak me out to have a second one found in one of my cemeteries."

Vanessa stared over toward the digging. "I bet. Let's hope that's not the case."

They fell silent as the coffin began its ascent from below ground.

137

LET'S PLAY

****

Jason's phone began to ring. "Strong."

"Jason, this is Eli."

"Hey, what have you got?"

"We just completed searching the second possible location for Rosalind Garner. The tech said the pattern here matches what he found where you are."

"Okay. Did you call Banks?"

"Yes. She wants to wait on your results before requesting another search warrant."

"Makes sense. I'll call her as soon as I know."

Jason hung up as the coffin cleared the hole and settled on the ground. He'd secured a ladder from Nathan and slid it into the hole. Climbing down and pulling on latex gloves, he used a small garden trowel to scrape away the dirt.

As he began to get deeper, his heart hammered in his ears. Locating the body Joann Heddon could help them find Tammy-Jo, but it also meant a phone call to Joann's parents, and the end of their hope. He focused on the task.

"Anything?"

He didn't look up at his partner but

138

answered while he worked. "Not yet."

Almost as soon as the words left his mouth, a piece of pink cloth appeared through the dirt. He tugged on it lightly and more followed. He knew what he was looking at and what it meant.

Vanessa saw it too. "Is that what I think it is?"

Jason stood, brushing the dirt from his knees. "It would appear so."

He climbed back out of the grave, removed the gloves, and dialed the Lieutenant.

"Banks."

"We've got a body."

There was a slight hesitation followed by an audible sigh. "Okay...I'll tell Doc Josie, and then I'll get Eli a search warrant. Stay by the grave and make sure nothing is touched."

"Will do." Jason hung up and looked for Nathan. Vanessa was already talking to him and it was obvious the news had shaken him up. Jason didn't care about the kid's feelings. He needed an answer to one question. He walked directly over, only waiting until he was in earshot, to blurt out the question.

"Nathan!"

"Yeah?"

"Is Immanuel Lutheran Cemetery one

139

of yours?"

Nathan was clearly intimidated by Jason's tone. "You mean do I manage it?"

"Yes."

"No. I don't even know where it is."

Jason stopped in his tracks as Vanessa gave him a confused stare. He nodded for her to follow him, which she did, after telling Nathan to stay put.

"What's up?"

"It appears likely that Nathan is not our guy."

Vanessa looked back at the kid, then at Jason. "How do you know?"

"The cemetery where Eli is digging for Rosalind Garner is Immanuel. Wolsey wouldn't have had the same access to it as he does the other two."

Vanessa thought about it before agreeing. "It doesn't make sense he would take a chance when he could use the cemeteries he is in charge of."

"Even so, let's keep him in the dark, just in case we're wrong."

"Agreed."

"I was thinking…"

"Did it hurt?"

"More than you know. Finding this body, assuming it turns out to be Joann Heddon, supports the pattern you suggested. That means…"

"Tammy-Jo Cousins has roughly thirty-six hours left," Vanessa finished.

****

The interior of the box was beginning to overwhelm Tammy-Jo's senses. The darkness was claustrophobic, the foam insulation around the sides was irritating her skin, and the smell of dried blood mixed with her own body odor was causing her to dry heave.

The box suddenly opened, washing her with a welcome breath of fresh air, but her relief was instantly followed by the rising fear that came with being in her captor's presence.

"A new game awaits us."

She didn't bother resisting, and sat up while shielding her eyes. "A new game?"

"Backgammon; have you ever played?"

She'd watched others play, but it had never appealed to her enough to learn how. "No."

"That's fine. Go to the bathroom and then I'll teach you."

She made her way down the hall, did her business, and then struggled back. In the beginning, she would stall for time in the

141

bathroom, but now thirst and hunger drove her to hurry.

The table was set as usual, but this time her food consisted of just toast and a half glass of water. She inhaled them. "Can I have more to eat?"

"No."

"How about water? Can I have another glass?"

"No."

The implication of his refusal slowly dawned on her.

He's not worried about me going without food or water.

When he began to explain the game to her, she found it nearly impossible to focus. Even though she felt safe in the box, she rarely slept. On top of being exhausted from her ordeal, thirst and hunger were constant companions.

"It's your turn!"

She jumped. "I don't know what to do."

"Weren't you listening?"

"Yes… I just don't understand."

"You weren't paying attention, I could tell. You know what? Let's forget this."

He threw the dice down onto the table. "Roll your first set of numbers."

"No, no…I want to play."

"Too late! Roll!"

She started to cry, barely able to produce tears, but sobbing anyway. She reached over, picked up the dice, and dropped them back onto the table. A two and a three. Even in the fog taking over her brain, she knew she was in trouble. Five could only be made by two combinations where seven had multiple sets of numbers.

He didn't bother announcing the roll. "Go again."

She did, and wasn't the least surprised when a six and one showed up. The excitement at the playing of the game from the previous nights was gone from his demeanor. His voice was cold, matter-of-fact, and emotionless.

"You lose; get up."

"No, please…"

This time he ignored his knife and reached over the table, grabbing her by the hair. She had nothing left to fight him with. He dragged her to the room and raped her.

Several hours later, she was returned to the box. There was no relief from being there, as she had known all along but denied to herself, she wasn't safe from him anywhere. The only thing different tonight was she no longer cared.

143

LET'S PLAY

CHAPTER 11

Jason and Vanessa arrived at the station the next morning acutely aware that it was day six. They had to find Tammy-Jo today.

Banks had called them last night to report Eli had found a body, presumed to be Rosalind Garner, and that she would be exhumed this morning.

The first stop for the detectives was Doc Josie's lab. She was ready for them when they came through the lab doors.

"Follow me."

She led them to the back of the lab and flipped a switch on a light panel. Two x-rays appeared before them. Doc Josie pointed as she talked.

"This one was provided by the family when Miss Heddon disappeared. This on the right is the one I took from the exhumed remains at Davenport Cemetery. See the fillings here, here, and here."

Both detectives nodded.

"We've got missing teeth in two locations, here and here, and the upper wisdom teeth have been removed in both cases. This is your girl, I'm afraid."

The news didn't surprise Jason, but he needed more. "What about cause of death?"

"You'll have to go see Doc Davis on that."

"Okay, thanks Josie."

"You're welcome."

They crossed the hall to the Morgue and found Darrel Chase washing down an autopsy table. "Hey, Darrel. Is Doc around?"

"He's putting a body in the freezer."

Right on cue, the freezer door opened, and Doc Davis came out. To Jason it looked like the doc was sweating. "Hot in the cooler, Doc?"

He laughed. "Not really." He turned to Vanessa. "I thought I told you not to bring him down here with you."

She shrugged. "I try, but he misses you."

Doc snorted. "I bet!"

Jason and Vanessa followed Doc as he walked into the tiny cubicle he called an office. Jason was anxious to find out the COD of Joann Heddon. "Did you finish with the Heddon autopsy?"

145

LET'S PLAY

Doc picked up a folder from his desk and handed it to Jason, who passed it to Vanessa, while he waited for the short version.

"Cause was a combination of blunt force trauma, blood loss, and suffocation. Which one was the determining factor is hard to say."

"The trauma, was it from a similar item, such as a hammer?"

"The wound is the same, so yes. The trauma and blood loss were a match to the Melinda Gomez autopsy, but suffocation was detectable in this case."

"She was alive when she was buried?"

"Technically, yes. I found inhaled soil particles in the throat and lungs, but whether she was conscious or not, I can't tell."

Jason pushed. "But it's possible she was alive when she was placed in the grave?"

"Unfortunately, I believe so."

"Thanks, Doc."

Jason turned and headed for the door as Vanessa scrambled after him. The elevator doors were opening when she caught up and followed him on. "You didn't hang around for the rest of the report."

"I figured you would tell me anything else important in the file."

"Why were you so interested in

146

whether Joann Heddon was alive when she was put in the grave?"

"Today is day six for Tammy-Jo, right?"

"Right."

"And if the timeline holds, he will try to bury her tonight, correct?"

"If it holds, yes."

"Well, I think our best chance to catch this guy is to stake out the cemeteries we consider a possible for tonight."

"Makes sense, but why the concern for her being buried alive."

The elevator doors slid open on the third floor, but Jason didn't walk out.

"Because it means Joann was alive when she got to the cemetery. We can only hope the same is true for Tammy-Jo."

****

He'd picked up the morning paper in preparation for that night. Passing the room with the box in it, he went into the third bedroom, flipped on the light, and threw the newspaper on the desk. Walking across the room to the opposite wall, he stared at the oversized map of San Antonio hung there.

Red pins were stuck in three places, each signifying a different location already

147

used, and green pins were stuck in each of the remaining cemeteries outside the city center. The green pins indicated potential burial sites for his girls, and he'd done recon at all of them, making sure they had enough seclusion.

He moved back to the desk, his pulse quickening with the job at hand.

Time to prepare for the burial of girl number four.

Pulling the funeral notices page from the Community section, he laid it onto a small desk, and ran his finger down the several columns listing the deceased. Each time he found the date April 7 listed for the funeral, he highlighted it with yellow.

When he was done, he moved back to each yellow marking and looked at the name of the cemetery. Checking it against his location map, any cemetery that had a green pin, got a green highlighter mark over its name in the paper. When he was done, there were three cemeteries that had both green and yellow highlighter marks.

Picking up his recon book from the desk, he found the name of each cemetery in his notes, reviewing his observations and picturing the location in his mind. The first cemetery didn't suit him, not for any particular reason, but just because he didn't like the name.

Scratch that one!

The second option seemed to be fine, and the third option was good as well.

How to decide?

A smile slowly creased his face.

I know the perfect solution.

****

Jason had the newspaper section with funeral notices laid out in front of him on the conference table. Vanessa had taped a map of the city and surrounding area up on the chalkboard. She stood back and examined what they had come up with. "Is that all of them?"

"That's all I've found. Patton and Banks are due here in a few minutes, so let's go over what we have."

"Okay. I see four possible locations for stakeouts."

"Yup. Kruestler Cemetery to the northeast, Saint Luke Cemetery south of the city, Becker Cemetery to the west, and San Isidro."

"You think we should eliminate San Isidro?"

"Yeah, so far he hasn't used the same cemetery twice, but maybe we send someone out there anyway. Just in case."

149

LET'S PLAY

"So, that gives us four to stake out tonight."

The door to the conference room opened. Patton and Banks came in and took seats without saying a word. When they were situated, Banks studied the map, then turned to Jason.

"Do you have a plan?"

"Yes."

"Good; let's hear it."

Jason began to explain the process by which they'd eliminated some and chosen other cemeteries when the captain waved his hand to stop.

"I've got a meeting with the mayor in twenty minutes. I'm afraid you'll have to cut to the end."

Vanessa took over and pointed with the end of a marker at one cemetery, then the next. "We have four cemeteries we want to stake out tonight. Kruestler, Becker, Saint Luke, and San Isidro."

"What assets do you need?"

"Three patrol cars and three EMT units. One of each within a mile of the three main stakeouts, ready to respond at a moment's notice, if our guy shows. We also need a fourth patrol car to watch San Isidro, just in case."

Patton glanced at Jason. "Why the EMTs?"

"We're hoping Tammy-Jo Cousins will still be alive when we find her, and if she is, we may not have time to wait for medical personnel to be called after the fact."

Patton let his gaze move around the room from the map, to his detectives, and finally settling on his lieutenant. "Sarah, I want you to be placed at a middle point and serve as task force co-coordinator."

Banks nodded.

Patton looked at his watch, then stood. "I'll sign off. Get it set up, and keep me in the loop."

"Yes, Sir." The response came in unison.

****

Tammy-Jo must have drifted into a semi-conscious numbness because, when the top of the box flipped open, she jerked with surprise.

He laughed. "Snuck up on ya, huh?"

She wiped at her eyes, trying to clear her vision, but didn't respond.

"Sit up, we have one more game."

Immediately, her pulse raced. "*One* more?"

"That's right."

151

LET'S PLAY

"Then I can go home?"

He laughed again, this time longer. She tried to pull herself up out of the box but he pushed her back.

"You don't need to get out for this one."

"Why? What's the game?"

He handed her a single die. "Roll it on the floor."

She stalled. "I thought you said the floor didn't count."

"Just roll it!"

"What am I trying to get?"

"This game is odds and evens. Odd is one place, even is another."

"Place for what?"

"For you."

"Is one of them home?"

"I can't tell you that. Now roll."

She sat looking at him, afraid to move.

"Roll!"

She flinched, causing the die to fall out of her hand. It rattled around on the floor for a second or two before stopping on five.

"Odd. That settles it."

"Settles what?"

"I told you, that's a secret. Lie down."

"But…"

He shoved her flat and dropped the lid closed. The lock snapped shut and he was gone.

152

LET'S PLAY

CHAPTER 12

Jason returned to the station just after six, having gone home for a short nap and to have dinner with his girls. Sandy was never happy when he had to work nights, but at least it wasn't like the last time he'd been undercover, when he was almost killed.

Vanessa, Eli, and Banks were already in the conference room when he came in, the tension in the room palpable, everyone recognizing the importance of the night. If they were going to catch this guy, tonight might be their best chance, and if they were going to save Tammy-Jo, tonight might be their *only* chance.

Banks nodded at him when he came in, then stood up next to the map, pointing. "Okay, let's get this thing going. Eli, you have the Kruestler Cemetery. You'll park here, and the backup team will park two blocks away, here."

Eli nodded and made a note on his

own copy of the map while Banks continued.

"Vanessa, you have Saint Luke. Set yourself up here, and the team will be three blocks away, here."

Banks turned to Jason. "You have Becker. The spot with best line of sight is here, but it's outside the fence, which means your reaction time will be slower than the others. The support team will be here, behind an old barn. We got permission from the land owner."

Jason pointed his pen at Banks. "And you?"

"I'll be here, just off the 1604 loop, less than seven minutes with lights and sirens, to each of your locations."

"What about response? What do you want the planned action to be if he shows up?"

"Once he has left the vehicle, and is near the grave, I want you to put yourself between the vehicle and him. As you move into position, call for backup. The black-and-white will join in the arrest; the EMTs will assess the girl."

Jason liked the set-up. "Sounds good. Is the other black-and-white set for San Isidro?"

"Yes. Vanessa, you and Eli are in secluded neighborhoods, and even though

155

your stakeout locations are inside the cemeteries, there's also likely to be civilians in the area. Don't get into a shootout if you can help it."

Eli nodded. "If our guy shows, do you want the other two detectives to move on the scene?"

"No. At least, not immediately. Let's make sure it's not a false alarm before we leave our posts."

The lieutenant looked around the room. "Any questions?"

Vanessa raised her hand, a tiny smirk appearing.

"Layne, what are you doing?"

"I have a question."

Banks stared at her, waiting.

"Will you be making deliveries from Starbucks during the stakeout?"

Anger seared the lieutenant's face until a smile broke out. Everyone laughed, a little of the tension relieved momentarily.

"Get your caffeine on the way to the stakeout, Layne! I don't do coffee runs."

****

Darkness was settling on West Texas a little later each day now. Jason thought the weather guy had said they were gaining four minutes of light every day, but out in the rural areas, street lights were absent, and darkness seemed to come on suddenly.

He'd arrived at his location, checked in with Banks, and slumped down in his seat. The clock on his dash glowed 9:10, and he assumed it would be at least midnight before this guy showed his face, but the nature of a stakeout was such that you never knew. One second you'd be fighting to keep your eyes open, the next moment, you could be fighting for your life.

His radio crackled, and he turned it down. In the stillness, it sounded like a megaphone. "Lieutenant, this is Vanessa."

"Go ahead."

"I'm in position, and I have my Starbucks."

Jason smiled in the darkness.

Man, that woman never gets tired of pushing the lieutenant's buttons. It's a wonder Banks doesn't have Vanessa working lost dog cases.

"Glad to hear it, Layne. Radio silence now unless you have something to report."

"Understood."

Jason had already heard Eli check in, as well as all four backup teams, and now it was a waiting game. He liked to pray at times like this, because it gave him hope, and it gave him peace. It also managed to

157

give him courage, which came in handy when on a stakeout.

For the next couple hours, the radio stayed silent.

****

Tammy-Jo heard the footsteps, but her mind no longer functioned well enough for her to be afraid. She had no strength to resist, no tears to shed, and no hope she would ever be free. Inside her box, she'd resigned herself to dying at the hands of the monster that held the key to her prison.

The lock snapped and the lid flew open. She covered her eyes with both hands, and as a result, she never saw it coming. One second there was bright light, the next a crushing pain, and then nothing.

****

Sarah Banks sat in the surveillance van, headphones on, listening for the first sign of their target. It was nearly midnight, and no indication they had guessed right. Normally, she enjoyed stakeouts. They broke up the monotony of her day-to-day routine, but that was before Gavin. She missed their time together when she had to work late.

Right on cue, her phone lit up with his picture. Slipping off the headphones, she pushed answer. "Hey there. I was just thinking about you."

"What a coincidence; I was just thinking about you."

"Sorry about this overnight duty, but I'll make it up to you, I promise."

"I look forward to it. Listen, I was thinking about what you said the other day."

"What I said?"

"Yeah, about keeping secrets?"

Sarah's heart thumped as her pulse quickened. "What about it?"

"I would never intentionally say anything, but…"

She waited.

"Somebody at the office may have overheard a conversation of ours."

"What makes you say that?"

"I was going back over some things in my head, and I remembered one of my associates leaning through the office door, waiting for me to get off the phone."

"What were we talking about?"

"That's the thing; I don't remember. I'm just afraid I may have said something that could hurt you."

Silently, she ran the possibilities through her mind.

LET'S PLAY

Don't be paranoid, Sarah. It's unlikely he said out loud anything relating to finding Gomez. You probably weren't even talking about the case during that conversation.

She tried to recall when they discussed the Gomez case, whether they were on the phone or together, but she couldn't remember.

"Sarah?"

"I'm here… It's okay, Gavin. I'm sure that wasn't the way the reporter got his information; things will work themselves out. I've got to go. I'll call you tomorrow and let you know how things went."

She hung up, hoping she sounded more confident than she felt.

****

He wiped the blood from the hammer and hung it back on the wall. Reaching into the box, he lifted the limp body out, and carried it to the garage. The back of his vehicle was already open, and he half-tossed, half-rolled the body forward, which fell with a deadened thump onto the carpet. Next to the body were the shovel, a stepladder, a pair of work gloves, and a small flashlight.

He closed up the vehicle, got in the

160

front seat, and triggered the garage door. A quick look at his watch told him it was 12:30. He was on schedule.

****

Vanessa tipped her coffee cup, expecting hot wake-up juice, but got nothing. She looked into the bottom of the cup.

"Crap!"

She keyed her microphone. "Lieutenant, you wouldn't happen to be near a coffee shop, would you?"

"Forget it, Layne."

Vanessa laughed.

"You can't blame a girl for try…"

Movement in the darkness stopped her. "Lieutenant, I've got movement here."

"Can you make an ID?"

"Not yet, but it's a solitary figure."

The radio fell silent, everyone waiting for a signal from Vanessa, hoping this was their guy. The figure moved toward the open grave, a thin flashlight beam illuminating his path. After several minutes, the lieutenant broke the silence. "Layne, what have you got?"

Careful not to make a sound, she slowly keyed her mic, whispering her

161

response. "It appears to be a man, and he's stopped near the grave. I'm going to get a closer look."

"Wait for your backup."

Vanessa lowered her window, and climbed out of her car, crouched low, waiting to make sure he hadn't heard her. The radio crackled again, much too loud with her window down. "Layne? Layne!"

The lieutenant's voice seemed to echo throughout the cemetery, and the man turned quickly in Vanessa's direction. She remained motionless, cursing herself for not turning off the radio, and waiting to see if the man moved. She poked her head up over the hood and spotted him peering at her, trying to see through the dark.

He didn't run, instead shining his flashlight in her direction. "Hello? Is someone there?"

Vanessa suddenly doubted this was their target. She stood up, her hand resting on her weapon, and approached.

"San Antonio police, identify yourself!"

The man's hands shot straight up. "Don't shoot. My name is Ross…Ross Tyner."

"Walk toward me, Ross."

The man came closer, and Vanessa saw for the first time the flowers he held in one hand. She relaxed, standing up and shining her flashlight at in his face.

"Mr. Tyner, what are you doing here?"

"I'm visiting my Molly."

"Your Molly?"

"Yes, she was my wife. I like to come in the quiet to speak to her."

Vanessa's heart broke. "I'm sorry to disturb that, but I need to see some ID."

"Of course." He rummaged around slowly in his coat pocket until he found his wallet. Vanessa looked at the picture on the driver's license and everything matched.

"I'm sorry to have disturbed you, Mr. Tyner."

"It's okay. May I go now?"

"Absolutely."

Vanessa returned to the car where she could hear Banks going ballistic. "Layne, dang you, answer!"

Blue lights flashed as the backup car responded to where Vanessa was.

"This is Vanessa. All clear."

"What do you mean, all clear? What happened?"

"The guy I saw was here visiting his dead wife."

"In the middle of the freaking night?"

"Yes."

"For crying out loud. Well, you might as well wrap it up; your cover is no doubt

163

LET'S PLAY

blown."

"Yes, ma'am."

****

He drove slowly through the gates, his eyes flicking back and forth, searching. His headlights were off, but the orange parking lights gave him sufficient light to see, and he soon made his way to the back of the cemetery. There, just off the road, was a mound of dirt and an open grave.

Looking back over his shoulder, he checked the girl. She remained motionless, and more importantly, quiet. He turned off the vehicle and got out. This time in April, the nights were still cool, and it made his work that much easier.

He checked the time; 1:30. He wanted to be gone within an hour.

Opening the back doors, he put on the gloves and grabbed the shovel. Running his arm through the rungs of the ladder, he lifted it onto his shoulder. The moon was bright enough that he didn't need the flashlight.

It's a beautiful night for doing some digging.

****

Jason pinched his arm. It was a tactic he employed to stay awake. Nothing did the job like a shot of pain, and he usually managed to bruise himself on these long stakeouts. They were to stay in position until sunrise, which this time of year, was around six in the morning. It was 1:30.

Jason sat upright, his eyes straining. An orange glow was moving through the cemetery.

Parking lights!

They stopped in front of the open grave, and a man came around to the back of a white minivan. When the doors opened, the interior lights didn't come on, so Jason couldn't be sure if Tammy-Jo was inside. What he did see was a shovel, followed by a ladder.

The man walked toward the open grave, dropped the shovel into the hole, and swung the ladder off his shoulder. Jason waited until the man disappeared into the hole.

"Lieutenant, this is Jason. I've got him; all units respond to my location."

With that, Jason jumped out of the car, drew his gun, and raced to the edge of the open grave. He snuck close enough to reach out and grab the ladder, jerking it out of the hole.

"Hey! Who's there?"

165

LET'S PLAY

Jason flicked on his flashlight. "San Antonio Police. You're under arrest."

Ricardo Bonitez, clawed at the sides of the hole, but there was no getting out. Jason held his light on the man until the black-and-white arrived. Once the officers were graveside, he raced for the van.

Throwing open the back doors, his flashlight fell on the motionless form of Tammy-Jo.

"Tammy! Tammy-Jo, can you hear me?"

Blood was dried in her hair and her eyes were partially open. He reached out and touched her throat, fearing cold skin, but was excited to find a faint pulse. The EMTs were just arriving.

"Over here! She's still alive!"

Jason stepped out of the way, letting the medical team do their work, as the night filled with sirens.

EPILOGUE

Jason sat across from Bonitez, who was cuffed to the table in the interrogation room. Jason watched him closely, but Bonitez refused to meet his stare, and otherwise seemed unfazed by his situation.

Jason closed the file folder in front of him. "Right now, you're looking at three counts of first-degree murder, four if Tammy-Jo Cousins dies, along with a slew of other charges. They're going to lock you up and throw away the key, but you might be able to avoid the death penalty if you cooperate and give a complete statement."

"Why would I do that? To make it tidy for you cops?"

"Do you want the chair?"

Bonitez finally looked up. "Fry me, I don't care."

"Why?"

"Why what?"

"These women didn't do anything to

167

you, so why?"

Bonitez gaze returned to the floor and his words were muffled. "My wife died last year and I needed somebody to play games with."

"I can't hear you."

"I needed someone to play games with!"

Jason had heard many motives for just as many horrific crimes, but this one sickened him.

"What about the women? They could've had husbands and kids who wanted to play games with them. You and your wife had that, but you took the chance away from them."

Bonitez didn't respond. In fact, he did his best to look bored.

Jason stood, opened the door, then turned around before leaving. "Bonitez."

"What?"

"If they give me the chance, I'll be there to throw the switch."

He let the door slam behind him.

****

Two days had gone by since the arrest of Bonitez and the end of the River Walk Missing case. John Patton had just got off the phone after speaking to Chief Williams. He got up from his desk and walked out of his office.

"I'll be down on the third floor, Mary."

"Okay, Captain."

He took the stairs and came out on the floor to find a circle of people, all standing, except for Jason. He was telling a story. Banks was in her office, so he nodded at everyone, and went in to talk to her.

"Got a minute, Sarah?"

She looked up, surprised. "Sure…sit down, John."

"No. This won't take long."

"Okay…shoot."

"I leaned on you pretty hard to find out if the story reported by that reporter had come from our department…"

"Yeah…"

"Well, I just got off the phone with Chief Williams."

"And?"

"He got a call this morning from the mayor. It seems that an aide who works at City Hall is a nephew of Devin James."

"You're kidding."

"Nope. Anyway, I wanted to make sure we're good."

"You know we are, John."

"Thanks, Sarah. I'll let you tell your team. By the way, what's the condition of

169

the Cousins girl?"

"She's still comatose. The blow from the hammer caused swelling in her brain. They think she'll make it, but don't know her long-term prognosis."

"Linda and I will be praying for her."

"I think a lot of people are."

****

Sarah sat at her desk, watching the captain walking toward the elevator while she tried to catch her breath. A load had been lifted and she could feel its absence. She picked up her phone and dialed Gavin.

"Hello?"

"Hey, it's me."

"What's up?"

"I just wanted to call and apologize for doubting you."

He was quiet for a minute. "That's not necessary, Sarah."

She smiled into the phone. "I love you, Gavin Newman."

"Right back at you, Miss Banks. Have you told your gang yet?"

"No, but I think it's time. See you later."

She hung up and went out to where the gathering was. Doc Davis, Doc Josie,

Vanessa, Eli, and Jason were all visiting and laughing. Jason was in the middle of a story.

"So, I'm sitting on the bed while Sandy is getting ready for work. She's in the bathroom and yells out, 'I'm late!' I look at my watch and she's got at least another forty-five minutes before she has to leave. 'You've got plenty of time,' I said."

"She comes out holding a stick and I ask her what it is, and she says it's a pregnancy test. And I'm like 'Oh, that kind of late!' and she laughs at me."

His eyes get huge as he tells the story. "Wait, a pregnancy test! You didn't tell me you thought you were pregnant. She says, 'I don't, but I figured I'd check anyway. These stupid things are so hard to read!' She walks over and gives it to me."

Jason pretended to look at the stick. "I looked down and it says plain as day in blue letters—pregnant—and I'm like, 'This isn't hard to read, it says you're pregnant.' And that's when I look up to see her standing there, grinning at me."

Everyone laughed at the look on Jason's face and took turns congratulating him on the news. Sarah went back to her office. She decided her news could wait a little longer.

LET'S PLAY

A NOTE FROM THE AUTHOR:

I can't begin to tell all of you who have written how much it means. Your encouragement has pushed me to finish now the tenth book in this series.

I hope you enjoyed it and that following the characters is still satisfying. If this is your first read in the series, thank you for taking the time, and I hope you will try the others, as well.

As always, I want to thank my wife Bev, for prodding me forward, and keeping me on task. Also, my editor Samantha, who fixes things without hurting my delicate ego. For that I'm grateful.

Please don't hesitate to write at mailto:jdalglish7@gmail.com or stop by my webpage at http://jcdalglish.webs.com/.

God Bless and hope to see you next book,

John

JOHN C. DALGLISH

MORE BY JOHN C. DALGLISH

THE DETECTIVE JASON STRONG SERIES

"WHERE'S MY SON?"- #1
BLOODSTAIN - #2
FOR MY BROTHER - #3
SILENT JUSTICE - #4
TIED TO MURDER –#5
ONE OF THEIR OWN – #6
DEATH STILL – #7
LETHAL INJECTION - #8
CRUEL DECEPTION - #9

THE CHASER CHRONICLES SERIES

CROSSOVER– #1
JOURNEY- #2
DESTINY -#3
INNER DEMONS - #4

Made in the USA
Middletown, DE
12 October 2017